"You don't have a job, Abby…let me provide you with one,"

Ethan said. "You can be Sona's nanny. Her governess. Her teacher. *My* teacher. Call yourself anything you want. But come to work for me. We *need* you."

Abby's heart lurched in her chest and her mouth went dry.

No, Abby, a tiny voice said. *Don't even consider this.*

"You don't know me," she pointed out.

"I know enough. I know you're the kind of woman who puts her whole life aside for two days in order to make a total stranger's dreams come true."

"B-but—"

"Abby…" The quiet desperation in his voice, in his gaze, sliced through the very words she was about to utter. "I *need* you."

ROMANCE

Dear Reader,

Happy New Year to you, and Happy Birthday to us! This year marks the twentieth anniversary of Silhouette Books, and Silhouette Romance is where it all began. Ever since May 1980, Silhouette Romance—and Silhouette Books—has published the best in contemporary category romance fiction, written by the genre's finest authors. And the year's stellar lineups across all Silhouette series continue that tradition.

In Romance this month, bestselling author Stella Bagwell delivers an emotional VIRGIN BRIDES story in which childhood nemeses strike *The Bridal Bargain*. ROYALLY WED, Silhouette's exciting cross-line series, arrives with *The Princess's White Knight* by popular author Carla Cassidy. A rebellious princess, her bodyguard, a marriage of convenience—need I say more? Next month, check out Silhouette Desire's Anne Marie Winston's *The Pregnant Princess* to follow the continuing adventures of the Wyndham family.

Plain Jane Marries the Boss in Elizabeth Harbison's enchanting CINDERELLA BRIDES title. In Donna Clayton's *Adopted Dad*, a first-time father experiences the healing power of love. A small-town beautician becomes *Engaged to the Doctor* to protect her little girl in Robin Nicholas's latest charmer. And *Husband Wanted—Fast!* is a pregnant woman's need in Rebecca Daniels's sparkling Romance.

In coming months, look for special titles by longtime favorites Diana Palmer, Joan Hohl, Kasey Michaels, Dixie Browning, Phyllis Halldorson and Tracy Sinclair, as well as many newer, but just as loved authors. It's an exciting year for Silhouette Books, and we invite you to join the celebration!

Happy reading!

Mary-Theresa Hussey

Mary-Theresa Hussey
Senior Editor

Please address questions and book requests to:
Silhouette Reader Service
U.S.: 3010 Walden Ave., P.O. Box 1325, Buffalo, NY 14269
Canadian: P.O. Box 609, Fort Erie, Ont. L2A 5X3

ADOPTED DAD

Donna Clayton

Silhouette
R O M A N C E™
Published by Silhouette Books
America's Publisher of Contemporary Romance

This book is lovingly dedicated to Sona Katy Powers,
a feisty Southern lady who has kept my life interesting.

Many thanks to Nona Baker, who resides in Slovakia.
Your patience in answering my "thousand and one"
questions is much appreciated.

 SILHOUETTE BOOKS

ISBN 0-373-19417-X

ADOPTED DAD

Copyright © 1999 by Donna Fasano

This edition published by arrangement with Harlequin Books S.A.

® and TM are trademarks of Harlequin Books S.A., used under license.
Trademarks indicated with ® are registered in the United States Patent
and Trademark Office, the Canadian Trade Marks Office and in other
countries.

Visit us at www.romance.net

Printed In U.S.A.

DONNA CLAYTON

is proud to be a recipient of the Holt Medallion, an award honoring outstanding literary talent, for her Silhouette Romance novel *Wife for a While*. Seeing her work appear on the Waldenbooks Series Bestsellers List has given her a great deal of joy and satisfaction.

Reading is one of Donna's favorite ways to wile away a rainy afternoon. She loves to hike, too. Another hobby added to her list of fun things to do is traveling. She fell in love with Europe during her first trip abroad recently and plans to return often. Oh, and Donna still collects cookbooks, but as her writing career grows, she finds herself using them less and less.

Donna loves to hear from her readers. Please write to her in care of Silhouette Books, 300 East 42nd Street, New York, NY 10017.

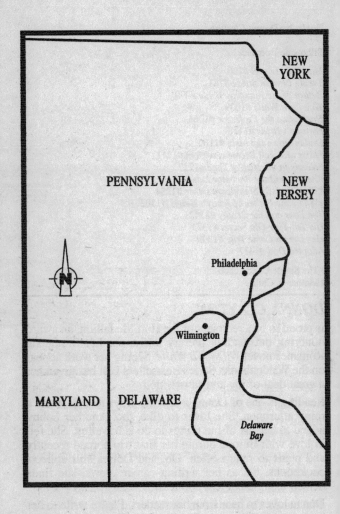

NEW
YORK

PENNSYLVANIA

NEW
JERSEY

Philadelphia

Wilmington

MARYLAND

DELAWARE

Delaware
Bay

N

Chapter One

"**W**hat do you mean, the rules have changed?"

Ethan Kimball tried hard to keep his irritation at bay as he questioned the foreign government worker. The scarred and chipped battleship-gray desk between them seemed as formidable as a brick wall. And it wasn't the only barrier separating them. The man didn't understand a single word of English, Ethan knew that. But his frustration was swiftly swelling into full-fledged, white-hot, scream-at-the-top-of-your-lungs anger. Wasn't anything going to go right here?

A dark cloud of dread seemed to descend on him in answer.

The man behind the desk—the person who held in his hands the power to grant or withhold Ethan's greatest wish—only shrugged. The guttural, Slavic language he spoke had Ethan automatically turning

to the third man in the small room, the young translator he'd hired named Viktor.

Ethan knew his impatience was showing. "What
is he saying, Viktor?" he asked, unable to quell the
sharpness in his tone.

"He asks your forgiveness," the translator replied,
his accent thick. "He says there is nothing he can
do. His superiors have decided that you cannot take
Sona from the orphanage. You cannot adopt her. You
cannot take the child from the country."

Each *cannot* struck Ethan like a boxer's swift jab
to the jaw. The overwhelming disappointment
wrenching in his gut was enough to make him want
to double over in agony. How could this be happening? All the problems were supposed to have been
ironed out *before* he'd left the United States. Now
here he was, halfway around the world, finding out
that his problems were only just beginning.

"I don't understand." Again Ethan addressed the
Kyrcznovian Child Services employee.

However, it was Viktor who explained further.
"You have no wife, Mr. Kimball."

"But everyone already knew that weeks ago! I
was told by the agency in the States—" Ethan lost
control, something he hated to do, but this stressful
situation was enough to send him through the roof.
He raised his voice and his speech became more an-
imated with the use of his upraised hands. "My being single wasn't supposed to be a problem! I was
told that the number of children made homeless by
the war was rising at a rate that caused a flexibility
of the law."

More conversation passed between Viktor and the

government worker, and in that instant, Ethan's eyes traveled down to the black-and-white photo he clutched in his fingers. He knew quite a bit about the toddler he'd come to Kyrcznovia to adopt.

The little girl depicted in the photograph was fourteen months old. Her dark brown gaze—"fearful doe-eyes" Ethan had dubbed them—clearly depicted a vulnerability that had affected him to an astounding degree. Her nut-brown hair had been hacked off at chin length. From all reports, she was healthy—or rather, she *had been* healthy when he'd applied for the adoption nearly a month ago. Not knowing how she fared at this moment was torturous. He ran a gentle finger down the edge of the picture.

Ethan wanted to be a daddy. No—he wanted to be *Sona's* daddy. Desperately.

The poor child had lost her parents when the couple had mistakenly walked across a small meadow just outside their border town that had been laced with land mines. *Kyrcznovian* land mines. Those two people couldn't have had a clue that they were taking their very lives into their hands, that their cutting across the field would leave their only child parentless.

This cute toddler—the child who had captured Ethan's heart from the moment he'd laid eyes on her picture—had been orphaned by "friendly fire," as the U.S. armed forces would have called it. The very idea made Ethan sick to his very soul.

Sona. His beautiful, lonely, *needy* little girl.

But these days in Kyrcznovia, Sona's story wasn't exceptional or unusual. So many children had been left hungry and homeless by the civil war raging in

the small, newly developing country that the government had made a plea. People all over the world were
called upon via the media to step up and help these
kids, to come forward and provide homes. And families...and love.

Kyrcznovia was a beautiful land, filled with cul-
ture and wonderful people. And Ethan was no
stranger to the country. He'd visited here, years ago,
when Kyrcznovia had been part of Russia, and his
parents had brought him abroad. He'd stayed in this
part of the country long enough to make friends. Of
course having been a happy-go-lucky twelve-year-
old at the time, Ethan had allowed himself to lose
touch with the boys he'd met. But he never forgot
the picturesque countryside.

At his home in Pennsylvania Ethan had been
watching the seven o'clock international news when
he'd learned of the plight of the children of war-torn
Kyrcznovia. Something deep inside him—something
he still didn't quite understand—had been stirred,
and he'd found himself dialing the toll-free phone
number on the television screen before he'd even realized it.

That had been weeks ago.

Working through an adoption agency in the States,
Ethan had first procured Sona's name. Then he'd received her file and photo. Slowly but surely all the
pieces had fallen into place. He'd even been told that
his dyed-in-the-wool bachelor status was no problem.
These children needed to be placed in good homes.
It mattered not that some of those homes would be
headed by single parents. The agency back in Amer-

ica had *guaranteed* that his being single would not stand in the way of his adopting Sona.

However, now he was discovering that the assurance he'd been given was wrong. Resentment-stirringly, ire-provokingly *wrong*.

"That may have been so—"

The sound of Viktor's voice had Ethan glancing up from the photo.

"—yesterday."

"Yesterday?" Ethan didn't even try to hide his angry disbelief. "And will you please tell me what could have happened in the short span of twenty-four hours that has changed all the damned rules?"

Viktor smiled. "Forgive me, Mr. Kimball. That was just…" He paused. "How do I say it…a figure of speech. I did not mean *yesterday* literally."

When Ethan didn't return the smile, the young man's humorous expression faded. "You see," Viktor continued, more seriously, "our country has just claimed its independence. Our government is just now being born. It is exciting. But there are… drawbacks. Our leaders are inexperienced. The rules here change from week to week." This time he couldn't stop his chuckle. "Sometimes from day to day."

Ethan saw that his chances of taking little Sona home with him were dwindling by the moment. Tension bracketed his mouth as he unwittingly pressed his lips together tightly.

"We will get it right," Viktor promised. "Eventually. But you must try to understand. Everyone involved is only trying to do what is best. The—"

"What is best?" Ethan raked his fingers through

his hair. "This man—" he indicated the Child Services worker sitting at the desk "—honestly believes that it's best for me to go home *without* Sona?"

After a silent moment, Viktor softly said, "He is not trying to do what is best for you. Our government is trying to do what is best for the children."

"Those children are hungry!" Ethan countered. "They're cold. They're scared. They're all alone in the world." Then he muttered in disgust, "Yet they're jammed into tiny, overcrowded rooms like…like little animals. There are twenty children for every adult caregiver in those orphanages. I've seen the reports. I know that—"

The man behind the desk spoke. And Viktor's response was so sharp, it had Ethan asking, "What? What did he say?"

Viktor shook his head at Ethan. "Nothing. He is only trying to lighten the mood. He made…how do I say it…a joke."

The sudden nervousness in the young translator's eyes caused the little hairs to raise on the back of Ethan's neck. Something was up. Something wasn't right. "It didn't sound like a joke," he said.

Viktor only averted his eyes.

"I'm paying you to translate," Ethan reminded the young man. There was a hint of warning in his tone as he said, "So translate."

"H-he said," Viktor stammered, "that for a hundred of your American dollars he would find you a young and sturdy Kyrcznovian wife. He said it would take him two days only. He suggests you go home with a whole new family."

At the sound of the word *wife,* Ethan's chin dipped

low and his whole body tensed. A permanent relationship was something he'd never have. Never.

"He meant no harm," Viktor rushed to say. "If you are not interested, he understands. However, if his superiors were to discover his offer, he would lose his job. Your discretion is much appreciated."

Ethan took a moment to steel himself before looking directly into Viktor's face, his own eyes reflecting a harshness he was simply unable to contain.

"As you said," Ethan replied, his jaw remaining tight and unyielding, "he was only making a joke." After giving the man behind the desk an unsmiling nod, he turned to leave.

"Mr. Kimball," Viktor called after him, "please remember that the rules could again change. Next month. Next week. Even tomorrow. Please do not be discouraged."

Discouraged didn't begin to describe how Ethan felt. He'd come too far, both in physical miles and in emotional commitment, to leave this country without that little girl. But he was devastated to realize that he had so little say in the most important matter of Sona's life, in the most important matter of his *own* life.

Ethan didn't bother responding to Viktor's encouragement. Instead he just kept walking down the dingy green hallway, his heart so heavy he felt as if it were a hunk of jagged lead sitting in his chest.

Abigail Ritter was in a fix. But she wasn't too worried about the situation. Sure, this turn of events was unexpected. But she'd been in this position before. Well...maybe not this *particular* position, with no job, no money and no prospects for either in anything resembling the near future. However, something would turn up. Some solution to her problem would soon present itself. It always did.

This hotel and its restaurant looked quite modern compared to the dozen or so others she'd visited this morning. She pushed her way through the door and scanned the room. Several customers sat at tables that had been meticulously lined into even rows. One dark-haired man, Abby couldn't help noticing, sat staring into his coffee mug as if he had the weight of the whole world on his shoulders. The clean, white tablecloths had a crisp stiffness that only plenty of starch and a hot iron could achieve. The floor was spotless, and so were the fresh white shirts of the staff. She wouldn't mind working in a place like this. At least, until she could make enough money to travel to her next teaching assignment.

Abby got the attention of a waiter and asked where she might find the man in charge. Without stopping on his trek toward the kitchen, the waiter pointed toward the back of the room. Her gaze followed his direction and she saw the door to what could only be the managing office. With purposeful steps, she made a beeline for it.

She smoothed her palms down the fabric of her skirt, rehearsing in her head her most persuasive arguments. She urgently needed a job. For if she didn't make some money soon, she'd be in deep trouble.

Shaking her head, she shoved aside the cloud of worry and focused instead on what she would say that would procure her employment here. She simply had to find a paying position for herself. Today!

* * *

The coffee in the heavy ceramic mug Ethan cradled between his palms was bitter and so strong that it had nearly burned away his taste buds since he'd been idling away his time here in the hotel's restaurant. The past four days since he'd stalked out of the Child Services department had been the longest of his life. The hours seemed to draw out into endless infinity. And in all of that time little Sona had never left his mind.

Was she hungry? Hurting? Frightened? Was she being watched closely in that overcrowded orphanage? Or was she being teased? Tormented? Abused?

Every single moment of not knowing was sheer agony for him. Were these the kinds of worries parents suffered for their children? Were these the fears a father felt…?

Something akin to a tap on his shoulder had his chin lifting, although no one was close enough to touch him. His gaze was automatically drawn to the woman making her way toward the back of the restaurant.

Her glorious head of long, wavy red hair was utterly striking. Her face was hidden from clear view, but he could see the rest of her…all five and a half feet of her feminine curves. He soon had a rear view, and the way her fanny gently swayed from side to side with each step was enough to make any red-blooded man salivate.

Ethan swallowed, his gaze darting down to his mug of cold coffee. Then he shot her another quick look, just in time to see her lift her balled-up hand and rap on the office door.

The woman participated in a fluid, unhesitating

conversation with the elderly man Ethan knew to be
the restaurant manager. However, even though she
spoke the language of Kyrcznovia, wore the same
clothing as other women he'd seen on the streets and
in the shops, there was still something...*off,* something not quite right about the scene he watched unfolding. But he couldn't put his finger on what it was.

When her tone turned urgent, and then pleading,
Ethan became openly riveted to what was taking
place between the man and woman at the far end of
the room. He heard her say, *"Prosím,"* several
times.

Now, Ethan didn't know much Kyrcznovian, but
during his daily visits to the Child Services building
with Viktor, he'd discovered how to pronounce
please perfectly...and he had. Many times.

The woman was obviously in some kind of trouble. She was either trying to explain her problem to
the manager, or she was begging him to help her
solve it. Ethan couldn't say which.

He wondered what misfortune she...

Blinking, he caught himself and stopped the
thought, midstream.

What was he doing? He shouldn't be wasting energy pondering someone else's dilemma. And some
woman's at that!

He'd made a solemn vow to himself years ago that
he'd make a berth around people of the female persuasion. A *wide* berth.

It was then that the manager firmly shut the office
door—right in the woman's face. The defeat and
weariness in her rounded shoulders had Ethan up and
out of his seat before he even realized it.

You will not speak to her, a stern voice told him. *You've got enough problems of your own. Walk right on by. The door to the rest room is just ten feet away. Head for it. Now!*

It was good advice. It really was. And he had every intention of following the silent commands the oh-so-logical part of his brain dictated. But just as he got near her, she heaved a heavy sigh and whispered, "Oh, my."

Ethan stopped in his tracks so abruptly that he had to lift his arms just a fraction to keep his balance. "You speak English."

At the sound of his voice, she reached up, tucked the silky tresses of her hair behind her ear and looked him full in the face. She gave him the barest hint of a smile, and Ethan felt as if he'd been clobbered over the head with a thick length of two-by-four.

This woman wasn't merely beautiful, she was gorgeous. She was young. Maybe in her midtwenties. Her wide-set eyes were the deep green of the rarest of emeralds, her tawny brows forming perfect wings hovering over them. Surely an exceptionally talented artist had delicately sculpted that tiny button nose and those high cheekbones.

Then his attention was totally captured by her lips...or rather, the flawless Cupid's bow of her upper lip. Hers was the most sensual, the most kissable mouth he'd ever seen in his entire life.

"You're..." he said in a husky whisper.

Stunning, he'd been about to say. But, thankfully, he was able to stop the utterance from rolling off his tongue.

He must be crazy! All this worrying and fretting

over his predicament with Sona had surely made him
take a tumble off the deep end into total insanity.

*You can't go around tossing out compliments to
complete strangers. In a foreign country, at that.
What on earth are you thinking?*

"An American?" she finished what she evidently
thought he'd been about to say.

Her smile widened a fraction as if to let him know
that she'd been approached plenty of times by people—just like him—who were surprised to find an
American dressing, speaking, *living* as any other native of Kyrcznovia. But he wasn't like all those other
people who had been taken off guard by her nation-
ality. He hadn't been about to comment on those
things at all. Instead, he had been about to make an
absolute fool of himself, and he'd be lying through
his teeth if he said he wasn't relieved that she had
mistaken his unfinished thought.

She softly added, "Yes, I am."

"Ah," was his only response. Several different
questions rolled through his mind at the same time.
What was she doing in the chaos of a brand-new
country? Didn't she know such political unrest carried danger for traveling foreigners? Where, in
heaven's name, had she inherited those exquisite
jewel-green eyes? Or rather, *from whom,* he guessed
was the correct turn of phrase...

Something in him stirred. Something deep. Primal.
At gut level.

He moistened his dry lips and tried to smile, but
for some unfathomable reason he couldn't get his
facial muscles to work. "You...ah, I..." he began.
But words failed him. Being this tongue-tied con-

fused him. After taking a quick, deep breath, he made another attempt. ''I couldn't help overhearing your, ah, conversation,'' he confessed. Then a small chuckle escaped from his throat. ''I don't speak the language, but...you seemed to be conveying that...you're in some sort of trouble.''

The inflection he placed on his observance put an inquiring twist on his statement. He wanted her to confide in him. That was the last thing he *should* have wanted at this moment. The very last thing. However, Ethan was simply too intrigued by the fiery-haired woman to listen to logic.

Abby couldn't help the earnest smile that tugged and then lingered on her lips. This man—this stranger—was expressing concern for her. And she was touched.

But what moved her most was realizing that this was the very man whom she had noticed studying his coffee with such focused, contemplative intent when she'd first entered the restaurant. She vaguely remembered making an unwitting assessment even then that he was obviously someone with a load of worries on his mind. However, here he was inquiring about hers. The idea was soul-warming to say the least, and it told her something about the man. Something important.

However, Abby wouldn't dream of adding to his problems by unloading hers onto him, too.

''Thanks for your kindness, but there's nothing to worry about.'' She hoped her appreciative tone let him see exactly how she felt about his concern for her. Reaching out, she touched him gently on the forearm—and was surprised speechless as a hot shock wave rolled across every inch of her skin.

She'd meant to assure him further that she'd be just fine. That her problem wasn't anything she couldn't handle. However, all she was cognizant of was the hardness of the corded muscles underneath the sleeve of his suit jacket. And the heat.

Her fingertips absorbed the warmth of his body and she felt suddenly feverish as the swelter fairly pulsed from him…and into her. Her skin flamed, from her neck and cheeks, all the way to the roots of her hair. It took every ounce of her strength to withdraw her hand from his arm.

"I—I'm," she stammered. Stopped. Swallowed. Then tried again. "I'm going to be fine."

But for the life of her she couldn't quite figure out if she was trying to reassure him—or herself.

Abby was mortified by her involuntary reaction to this man. A complete and total stranger. Things like this didn't happen to her. Surely, he must think she was some kind of forward floozy who…

At that moment, the low growl of a hunger pang rumbled from her tummy, further embarrassing her. She automatically pressed her hand against her stomach and murmured a quick, "Pardon me."

The corners of his mouth curled, but there wasn't a hint of teasing in his deep mahogany eyes when he said softly, "I'd like to invite you to lunch, but—" he shrugged "—I don't even know your name."

His gaze seemed to hold her spellbound. "Abigail," she responded, her voice sounding very far away to her own ears. "Abby Ritter."

She found herself helplessly studying his ruggedly handsome face—the wide, sexy mouth that smiled so charmingly, his clean-shaven jaw, his perfect, blade-like nose, those deep-brown, intense eyes fanned with dark lashes and thick brows, and finally his high forehead, feathered with light worry lines. His hair was the color of strong, rich coffee; its satiny texture glistened in the afternoon light. One errant lock curled downward and she had to fight the urge to reach up and comb it back with her fingers. He was a startlingly handsome man.

Suddenly realizing that her breath had become shallow, and worse yet, that she was staring, she took a quick, deep breath, blinked twice and averted her gaze.

Marvelous man that he was, he picked up the conversation as if the too obvious lag had never occurred.

"Well, Abby," he said easily, "let me buy you lunch."

"Oh, no." She shook her head. "I couldn't impose—"

He cut her off. "Nonsense. It would only be an imposition if you were keeping me from something, or if I had to be somewhere." Then his face grew strained as he added, "The truth is, Abby, you'd be offering me a respite…"

She studied him intently, sure he was about to reveal some tidbit of information regarding what was troubling him. But he didn't.

"…if you were to let me buy you something to eat."

Abby knew she shouldn't even consider his offer. He was nice man. A nice, handsome man. A man who didn't need to listen to her woes. And besides that, she needed to find a job. Today. And she wouldn't find any success in dawdling here with this nice, handsome man.

Another low rumble resounded from her stomach, and they both smiled in unison.

"What do you say, Abby?" he asked, his tone charming. Inviting. *Alluring.* "Will you have lunch with me? Will you tell me what's troubling you?"

She sighed. She *was* hungry. And letting him buy her a meal would be a solid financial decision on her part, wouldn't it?

"Only if you'll tell me your name," she said. "And...if you'll tell *me* what's troubling *you.*"

He told her his name was Ethan Kimball, and the look of surprise that had invaded his features remained staunchly in place until they were seated at the table, menus in hand.

"So, how did you know?" he finally asked.

She grinned. "That you have problems of your own?" One of her shoulders lifted a fraction. "Guess you could say I'm the observant type."

He nodded, seeming to accept the explanation.

Then she decided to be completely honest. "When I came through the door, I saw you studying your coffee mug like it contained some deep, enigmatic secret that you were bent on discovering."

Ethan chuckled, and Abby was sure it had to be one of the most pleasant sounds she'd ever heard.

"I see," he told her.

The waiter took their orders, and then Ethan asked, "So, what was that between you and the manager of this place?"

The sigh Abby expelled sounded tired, even to her. "He was turning me down for a job. It's very hard for a female to find employment in Kyrcznovia."

He frowned. "Well, what are you doing in the country without employment? How do you survive?"

"Oh, I had a job." Then she grimaced. "*Had* being the operative word. You see, I was teaching several groups of children English. The new Kyrcznovian government officials wanted to offer their children—*their future*—a better education. That was something the 'mother country' could never afford to give them, so that was part of the new leaders' primary plans. And I was part of that plan. Me and about a dozen other English teachers." She raised her brows, lifted her palms. "But that all changed yesterday when the funds for the program were suddenly cut off." Her tone dropped to a grumble as she added, "They probably needed money for the new army or something."

"Did you have a contract?" he asked.

"Of course. But it's only as good as the piece of paper it's written on."

"But surely something can be done."

The passion in his outrage for her plight made her insides grow all warm and fuzzy. Ethan Kimball really was a nice man.

"Surely they can be made to hold up their end of the deal they made."

Abby nodded. "I could fight it. But that takes money. Lots of money. And more time than I have. I've decided the best thing for me to do is cut my losses. Find another job. Earn enough money to cover the travel expenses to my next teaching assignment."

"Which is where?"

The grin she tossed him was a sheepish one. "I have to find it first, then I can tell you where."

He shook his head. "But—"

"Look, it's okay," she assured him. "I've been traveling Europe, teaching English for five years. Ever since I graduated from college. This kind of thing has happened before. Not so suddenly, maybe. But it's happened. I'll survive. Something will turn up."

Creases of skepticism marred his forehead, and she was sure he was going to argue with her, but the waiter interrupted them with plates of food.

Scooping up a forkful of *halusky,* she commented, "Well, you know my troubles. Now it's your turn."

Before she even had time to chew the small potato dumplings, she was holding a picture of Ethan's "little girl" as he called the child he'd traveled halfway across the globe to adopt. Abby listened as he summed up his story as quickly as possible; how he'd been told back in the States that his bachelor status was no problem, how he'd discovered the rules had changed, how he'd been encouraged to remain in the country with the hope that the government's dictum would be reverted once again. Finally, Abby had to place her fork on the table. The knot of emo-

tion that had formed in her throat made it impossible
for her to swallow.

"I don't know, Abby." His voice was a mere
whisper. "I own my own business and that's why
I've been able to stay these extra days. But I can't
let my company go to hell in a handbasket. I just
don't know how much longer I can wait for Child
Services and the government to get their acts together. I go to see them twice a day. I explain to
everyone who will listen that it's in Sona's best interest to go home with me." He shook his head.
"But, so far, I haven't convinced anyone."

The pain and worry in his dark eyes was heart-
wrenching to her.

"Have you seen her?" Abby asked. "Have they
let you spend time with Sona?"

Ethan shook his head, and his anxiety seemed to
grow. "They say the adoption is too much in question to allow us to meet. To bond. They say they are
only trying to spare the both of us the pain of separation. I understand. But, Abby, I already have a
bond. An emotional bond that started weeks ago. I'm
already suffering the pain of separation."

His jaw clenched then, and just before he averted
his gaze, Abby was sure she saw his eyes misting.
This man was hurting. Badly. All for the sake of a
little girl who probably didn't even know of his ex-
istence.

Yet.

His story, his *suffering*, roused something inside
Abby. Something she couldn't quite figure out.
Something that moved her to act—swiftly, mind-

lessly—before she even had time to contemplate the consequences of her behavior.

"Well, Ethan." The nerves jittering in her belly made her voice come out sounding weak and shaky. "If all you need is a wife, then I'd be happy to marry you."

Chapter Two

Abby could not believe the words that had just somersaulted right out of her mouth. She'd parted her lips and the offer had twirled and flipped, making a perfect execution like an outstanding Olympic gymnast.

Oh, she knew why she made the suggestion of marriage. Her motivation couldn't have been more clear to her had it been the bright and blazing summer sun rising over the wild Kyrcznovian landscape. Abby took a quick peek at the little girl's photo. Sona. The dark-eyed toddler was all alone in the world. The mere idea stirred highly emotional memories in Abby. Memories that threatened to bring tears to her eyes, swallow her whole, if she were to tarry in them long enough. Blinking, she shoved her way out of the dark thoughts.

Abby didn't know Sona, had never met this tiny

moppet, but Abby felt an affinity for her nonetheless. If Abby could help rescue one lonely soul…

This time her tone was stronger as she repeated, "I'll be happy to marry you, Ethan."

He didn't speak, his wide mahogany eyes staring in disbelief. He was evidently as stunned by her offer as she. More so, even.

She suddenly felt buoyant, certain she was doing the right thing. "Gee," she said, trying to fill the awkward silence, "it's not like I'm offering to become your lifelong partner. You only need a wife for a while, right? Just long enough so that you can adopt Sona." She grinned. "Then we'll get one of those quickie divorces that some of those states in America are famous for." She lifted her hands, palms up. "Couldn't be more simple, don't you think?"

It took him several moments to respond. Finally, he said, "Why? Why would you offer to do this, Abby? You don't even know me."

The intensity in his dark-brown eyes made her uncomfortable. "It's nothing," she told him, wanting to sidestep his profound query.

He reached across the table and took her hand in his, and the heat of his skin sent concentric shivers coursing across every inch of her flesh.

"It isn't nothing," he said quietly. "It's something. Something big. Bigger than you can ever imagine."

His fingers were strong as they clasped hers, and Abby's heart began to race.

"So, tell me," he pressed. "Tell me why you would make such a monumental overture."

With her free hand, she swiped her fingers through her bangs and shifted her gaze to glance off across the dining room. These were nervous gestures, meant only to give her time to think before she spoke.

Ethan wouldn't understand her motives. Then again, maybe he would. But did she really want to expose that much of herself to a total stranger? She didn't think so.

If he decided to take her up on her offer, then they would marry, she would go with him to pick up his new daughter, she might even go with them to the airport. However, soon, he and the little girl were going to fly off toward the West in a big plane...and Abby would never see him again. So why should she bare the most painful part of her past to him?

She shouldn't, she decided, pressing her lips together in a thin line. Inhaling deeply, she leveled a cheerful gaze on him.

"Look, I can help you," she said simply. "So, let me."

Ethan let out a small chuckle. "You know, the man from Child Services who rejected my adoption request offered to find me a 'sturdy wife'...for a fee, of course. A measly hundred bucks. Is that all a sturdy wife is worth these days?"

Abby's mouth dropped open a fraction in horror and surprise.

"I turned him down," he continued, his voice flattening. "You see, years ago I decided I wasn't going to get married." His jaw tensed and his gaze clouded over as he added, "Ever."

Remaining utterly still, she silently wondered what could have happened to force him to come to such a conclusion. *Years ago,* he had said. Yet he seemed young. Older than she, of course, but still young. Early to midthirties, she guessed. Seemingly too young to be tainted against loving relationships and lifelong commitments. What had he been through to cause him to—

Ethan chuckled again, evidently launching himself out of his fleeting-yet-all-absorbing moment of sadness. "However, marrying for the sole purpose of adopting Sona. Now, *that* I would do."

A few seconds of acute silence had them both feeling awkward.

"I think it's called a marriage of convenience," Abby said, forcing her mouth to curl into a smile.

"So, what's in this for you?"

His question took her off guard. She blinked. "For me?"

He nodded. "*If* I agree to this—and I'm not yet sure I do—how can you benefit? What can I do for you in return?"

Straightening her spine, Abby pulled her hand from his. "I don't expect to benefit."

"But how fair is that?"

"Who said life is fair?" Her chuckle didn't hold much humor. "The predicament I'm in right now pretty much answers that question."

"Oh, yes," he murmured. "Your predicament. Hmmm…how about if I pay you for your trouble?"

Abby's tiny jerk was totally involuntary, as if she'd taken a quick slap on the cheek. "I will not take money from you. That's not why I made the offer."

Lifting his hands, he rushed to assuage the insult

he'd inflicted. "I wasn't suggesting you had." Ethan reached up and toyed with his chin. "Okay…how about—" he spoke slowly and softly, as if he were voicing an idea as it formulated in his head "—if you let me foot the bill for all your travel expenses to your next teaching assignment? Plane fare, hotel, meals, the works."

"Oh, no." She leaned away from him, shaking her head. "I couldn't allow you to do that. It's too much."

"Nonsense. If it's going to be a true marriage of convenience, then it has to be convenient for us both, right?"

"B—but—"

She continued to protest, but he silenced her with a firm, upraised hand. "No buts," he said with a great deal of adamancy. He rested his elbows on the table. "Abby, I've been sitting in this hotel for *days*. I had just about given up. You've given me hope. You've made an offer to make my dreams come true. If you do this, you'll make me a father. *Sona's* father. Don't you realize what that means? To me *and* to that little girl. You've got to let me compensate you in some way. Travel expenses is the least I can do. The *least*."

He was persuasive, Abby thought. With his talk of fulfilling dreams and becoming a father. Yes, he was very persuasive, indeed. Finally, the stiffness in her shoulders eased and she smiled.

"Well," she said softly, "I didn't really want to spend the next couple of months working as a waitress, anyway."

His eyes sparkled with excitement, and Abby felt

a thrill shoot through her at the thought that she was
the one who had caused it.

"I can't believe it, Abby," he said. "I'm really
going to do it. I really am."

The thrill she felt magnified a hundredfold. His
sudden elation over tying the knot, after he'd so ada-
mantly proclaimed his aversion to matrimony, made
her feel all sunny inside.

"I really am going to be Sona's father."

Abby's mouth went suddenly dry with disappointment. Of course, his excitement had been spurred by
the anticipation of adopting his little girl. Abby was
silly to have thought anything else.

"Yes," she said, doing everything in her power to
stir up a little excitement of her own. "And I've
found the means to get to my next teaching assignment. Wherever that will be."

His sexy mouth widened into a grin and he
reached out his hand to her. "So, we have a deal?
We're going to help one another?"

With only the merest hesitation, she took his hand
and shook it. "Yes, we are," she agreed.

An odd cloud had descended on her, and where it
had come from she hadn't a clue. She had found a
solution to her problem. The answer had come. Just
as she knew it would. And with that solution came
the opportunity to help someone. She should be feeling happy. Joyous. But she didn't. What she felt was
a strange, hovering melancholy. And that confused
her.

"Ah, love is so…how do I say it…*grand!*"

Abby had only just met Viktor, the Kyrcznovian

translator Ethan had hired when he'd first arrived in the country. The young man had agreed to attend their wedding ceremony and act as the necessary witness. She found Viktor to be a tad too high-spirited. Of course, her opinion could have been colored by the doubt she was experiencing, along with the rethinking she was doing, regarding her participation in this scheme. Was she *really* doing the right thing in marrying a perfect stranger? Of course she was.

But then Viktor gleefully proclaimed to the world at large, "Love is wonderful."

The man's boisterousness—all his talk about love—grated on Abby's already frayed nerves. And from what she could see, Ethan was becoming just as agitated.

"I told you, Viktor," Ethan said, his tone flat, abraded, "this has nothing to do with love."

Viktor's voice lowered as he said, "But, Mr. Kimball, it is to invite…how do I say it…ill omens to have a wedding day and not speak of the most powerful of emotions." After a momentary hesitation, he continued, "It does not have to be *your* love that I proclaim. It can belong to someone else. But it is only customary to exalt and glorify love and affection and devotion—" he lightly thumped himself on the chest "—all matters of the heart, on a day such as this."

The fog that had hovered over Abby during each and every one of the forty-eight hours that made up the official waiting period grew denser by the moment. Ill omens and a loveless marriage. Boy, that summed up this situation perfectly.

Why was she feeling so…doomed? she wondered.

It just didn't make sense. Glancing at Ethan, she saw that the apprehension that plagued him had him antsy, too.

Viktor plowed ahead, ever joyous. "Look there." He pointed at a man and woman sitting on a nearby bench. "There is love and commitment in the way they are holding hands. And there." He indicated another couple. "The kiss they are sharing is sweet and pure." Viktor threw back his head and inhaled heartily. "Ah, yes, love is very grand."

Ethan only tossed him a frown.

"Ill omens," Viktor warned in a singsong voice. "And since you are not having the traditional celebration—"

"Those parties can go on for days," Abby couldn't help but interject.

"—you must at least agree with me on this," Viktor insisted.

After an impatient sigh, Ethan buckled. "Yes, Viktor," he said, "love *is* grand. Does that fulfill custom?"

Viktor sighed. "It will have to do." Then he raised his brows at Abby, waiting for a response from her.

"You're pressing your luck now," Ethan grumbled at the young man.

All Abby could muster was a tight-lipped smile. What did they expect from her? She was getting married…without fanfare, or flowers, without rings or a frilly dress.

Even her plastic smile faded at *that* thought.

What was the matter with her? She and Ethan had decided that keeping things simple would be the best way to go. Fanfare and flowers, rings and a frilly dress were for people who wanted to show their family and friends how they felt about each other. She didn't love Ethan. He didn't love her. She knew that. So what was the problem?

But, a tiny voice complained, *didn't a woman have a right to expect a little hoopla on her wedding day?*

No, came a firm, silent answer, *she did not. Not under these circumstances, she didn't.*

As they went into the building that housed the Marriage Office, Abby plastered the artificial smile back into place. The hallway was long and poorly lit, but she and Ethan knew their way as they had come here to register the very same day she'd offered to marry him. The office was busy then, just as it was busy now.

It seemed that the spirits of the citizens of Kyrcznovia were not in the least dampened by the civil unrest going on around them. On the contrary, the people of this country were very enthusiastic about the birth of their nation, and they were showing their ebullience and excitement in many different ways. Getting married seemed to be one of them.

Abby, Ethan and Viktor were told to take a seat.

Sitting in the overcrowded waiting area among all the laughing, affectionate couples, Abby could clearly see that love was the main reason these men and women had come here. Of course, there were at least a dozen other reasons why people got married. She'd lived in enough diverse cultures to know that. There were some countries where matches were still made by the parents of the young people who married. Those were more like lifelong business relationships, although many of the men and women eventually ended up developing a deep affection for the mate chosen for them. The women in those marriages might not have begun those unions feeling loved, but surely they felt needed...*wanted*.

That one little word was enough to turn Abby cold. A shiver actually coursed through her, and panic set in. It was then that she felt Ethan's intense brown eyes on her. She lifted her gaze to his.

Although there was no way he could know her thoughts, he evidently perceived something disturbed her. Maybe he would graciously decide to refuse her offer. Maybe it wasn't too late for her to get out of this...this foolish arrangement.

Ethan looked distraught. He leaned close, whispering in her ear. "I know you're having second thoughts. I've sensed it all morning. And I feel just awful about it."

After momentarily averting his gaze, he sighed and looked her full in the face. "But if we don't do this...if we don't go through with this marriage, they're not going to let me have Sona."

The second the little girl's name passed his lips, Abby reached out and touched his forearm. "It's okay," she assured him, not feeling at all assured herself. "I'm just a little nervous is all. I'll be fine."

His smile was small but his gratitude was as clear as the finest crystal.

It wasn't long after their brief conversation that they were called before the man who would marry them—the Kyrcznovian equivalent of a U.S. Justice of the Peace. The nagging cloud of doubt and anxiety never left Abby, although she was too busy explaining to Ethan all that was being said to focus on her uncertainty. When the officiant asked them if they both were before him of their own free will, Abby softly said, *"Ano,"* and then prompted Ethan to answer yes also.

Even Viktor had questions to answer about the couple.

There was one lighthearted moment when Ethan became a little tongue-tied with the Kyrcznovian words that had him "pledging his troth" to Abby. Everyone chuckled, and after a second attempt, Ethan got it right. Finally, they were pronounced man and wife.

"Well—" Viktor nudged Ethan with his elbow "—kiss her, why don't you?"

The whole room grew utterly still. Her new husband turned to face her, then he looked from the *Sobash uradnik,*—the man who had wed them—then to Viktor and then finally back to Abby. For a moment, she thought he meant to forgo this particular wedding ritual. Her stomach churned, her gaze darting from his questioning eyes, to his lips and then back to his eyes.

She was desperately afraid he would kiss her. She was also desperately afraid he would not. And the opposing confusion and chaos of these thoughts had her mind whirling a mile a minute.

Ethan leaned toward her, and suddenly his mouth was pressed to hers. His lips were firm, yet gentle, warm and—

The kiss was over almost before it began. She felt both relieved and utterly bereft. Lord, she'd never experienced such a jumble of emotions in her whole life.

"Let's go." His whisper was rough against her ear.

In a fog-filled tunnel, Abby felt as if she were in the throes of an out-of-body experience as Ethan shook the hand of the *Sobash uradnik,* smiling tightly at the man's proffered wishes for a lifetime of happiness in a language he didn't understand. After accepting some papers from the man, her husband took her elbow and steered her toward the door.

Her *husband...*

Abby took a deep breath. She felt so light-headed, so shaky.

This was ridiculous! She shook the thoughts from her mind. She was making too much out of all these silly feelings swirling around in her brain, in her chest. But her emotions were so surprisingly strong. And thick. They seemed to congeal in her lungs, making it hard for her to breathe.

Abby and Ethan burst through the door, into the bright sunshine. Abby gulped in the afternoon air, trying hard to keep her composure.

"The people at Child Services are expecting us," Ethan told Abby. "You will come with me?"

"Of course," she said.

He turned to Viktor. "Well, my friend...I want to thank you for helping me."

"This sounds like...how do I say it...a goodbye."

Ethan shrugged. "Abby can translate for me, so I thought—"

"Oh, no," Viktor protested. "I want to stick with you until the end. I want to meet that little girl."

The excited anticipation glittering in Ethan's eyes thrilled Abby and dissolved all her dark, ominous feelings. This man's dream was about to come true. She couldn't blame Viktor for wanting to be present when it happened. She was pleased to be a part of it, herself.

"Well," Ethan told them both, "let's go get my daughter."

He paced the length of the room and back. "What's taking them so long?" Ethan asked. "The paperwork for the adoption has been in order from the beginning. All they wanted was for me to have a wife. I have one. So what's the hold up?"

Concern and commiseration etched lines in Viktor's young face as he looked at the clock on the wall.

Abby let her gaze follow her husband's every move. She feasted on the sight of him. After today, she would never see Ethan again. She wanted some memories to take with her when they parted.

She wasn't stupid enough to believe that she'd fallen in love with Ethan Kimball since meeting him in that restaurant a couple of days ago. Why, he was really still a stranger to her. All she knew was that he loved a little girl he had never even met. And that had been enough to convince Abby that he was one extraordinary man. A man she wanted to help. And she had. She should feel good about that. So why then did she feel so conflicted?

"Do you think they're questioning the marriage?" he asked.

The fear in his eyes tore at her soul. "Why should they?" Lowering her voice, she remarked, "They have no idea that the two of us made a...a—" her tongue tripped over the word "—bargain." However, she had no clue what was actually happening behind the closed door of the office.

"They have sent someone to fetch your little girl," Viktor said, his tone more confident than his gaze reflected. "I am sure of it."

Ethan continued his pacing; Abby turned back to staring out the window.

The door of the waiting room opened, and the man from Child Services walked in with a dark-haired toddler in his arms. He crossed the room and wordlessly handed the child over to Ethan. The air was so still, so silent. Abby could hear her own heart beating like a huge kettledrum.

"Sona."

The euphoria in Ethan's whisper sent a chill racing up Abby's spine. Joy and relief made his gorgeous dark eyes shine with welling moisture, and Abby had to press her fingertips to her lips to keep from crying. Viktor, too, was highly emotional, his Adam's apple bobbing in his throat.

More paperwork was exchanged, and finally, the government employee bid Ethan a curt congratulations and he left them.

Viktor came to Ethan and Sona, smiled softly at the little girl, touched her on the chin. "You're a lucky little girl," he said to her. "I wish you much happiness, Mr. Kimball."

"Thanks for everything, Viktor." The two men shook hands.

"If you are ever in my city again, you be sure to…how do I say it…look me up."

Ethan nodded. "You can bet I will."

After tossing Abby a wave of farewell, Viktor closed the door softly behind him.

A moment of awkward silence followed. Abby saw that Sona looked uncertain, and she thought that was a very natural thing for the child to be feeling. This lovely dark-eyed little girl might feel lost right now, but Abby knew it wouldn't be long at all before Sona's gaze would shine with adoration and love when she looked at Ethan. The two of them would develop that strong father-daughter bond. Abby was sure of it.

Approaching Ethan, Abby said, "You want me to walk you back to your hotel?"

He shook his head. "I'm going to wait here awhile. I want to give her time to get used to me."

Abby hid her disappointment behind a smile. "I understand." He wanted time alone with Sona. That was clear. "You're going to be a fabulous father, Ethan Kimball."

Then he did something wholly unexpected. He reached up and gently caressed her cheek. The moment was poignant, special, and she savored every delicious second.

"This wouldn't have happened without you, Abby."

Her smile broadened. "I was happy to help."

"You have my business card," he said. "You call me as soon as you find a teaching assignment. I'll see that you get there. First-class."

His unexpected generosity made her chuckle. "Aw, but I'm not a first-class kinda girl."

"Oh, yes you are, Abby Ritter."

Her smile waned when he used her last name. She

felt a funny kind of sadness to realize he didn't think of her as his Mrs. But that was silly. Why should he?

"You're most definitely first-class."

She only stared at him for a moment, languishing in the warmth of his touch. And for an instant, she felt needed. *Wanted.*

The emotion that bombarded her was enough to make fresh tears spring to her eyes. Her eyelids prickled with the welling moisture, splintering his image into a thousand shards of watery light.

Stepping away from him, she dashed the tears away before he could see her reaction. This wasn't about her. It was about Ethan. It was about Sona.

After clearing her throat, she said, "I'm only glad I could help."

She looked from him to the little girl, and leveled her gaze on Ethan's face once again. Then and there, she knew that she'd done the right thing in marrying this man, in helping him adopt this beautiful, needy child. Abby was sure of it.

Reaching out, she captured Sona's fingers in hers. "Your daddy's going to give you a good life." She then repeated the words in the child's native dialect.

A shadow of a smile tilted the child's lips for a fraction of a second before the cloud of confusion and fear returned to her expression with a vengeance. Sona would be okay, Abby was certain of it. With a loving father like Ethan, how could she be anything else?

Abby's gaze was helplessly drawn to Ethan. For

some strange reason, she didn't want to go. But it was time.

Unable to bring herself to say goodbye, she simply offered him a smile. And then she left him alone with his new daughter.

Chapter Three

There simply wasn't a more adorable, more precious child in all of the whole wide world. Ethan might be exhausted from his day, but as he sat on the one chair in the cramped hotel room, his heart pounded furiously in his chest, emotion lodged firmly and thickly in his throat.

This was real. His dream had finally come true. He was a daddy. He was Sona's daddy.

His jaw clenched as he forced back the overwhelming disbelief threatening to engulf him. He needed to keep himself composed, relaxed. For Sona's sake. Several times since they had left the Child Services office earlier today, she had been on the verge of crying. Her tiny chin would quiver, her eyes had grown fearful and teary, yet in each instance he had been able to divert disaster by distracting her. Quickly. With whatever had been close at hand—a small chip of ice from his cup, a spoon from the dinner table, the new rattle he'd purchased for her. Boy, keeping Sona's mind occupied with new and interesting things was hard work.

But even with the difficulties, he was unable to get over how happy he felt at this moment, how completely joyous he'd been since the moment Sona had been placed in his arms. This adoption felt so right to him. So very right.

His daughter sat on the roll-away bed he'd had brought in by the hotel housekeeping. There hadn't been a crib available. Ah, well, he'd thought, they only had to make do for one night. They would be flying home to America—tomorrow.

Sona played with the new rattle, turning it this way and that, smiling tentatively whenever it made a noise. The inexpensive toy enthralled her, and Ethan could easily see that she hadn't had access to many playthings in the orphanage.

He'd taken her shopping for a few things: two bottles, a new dress, a little nightgown and, of course, some diapers. He'd also bought her some toys. Just a few small, colorful items. He didn't want to have to carry a lot of stuff on the airplane. But his own favorite was the small, redheaded doll he'd bought...a doll that reminded him of Abby.

Several times this afternoon the woman had breezed into Ethan's thoughts. His gratitude for what she had done for him was so immense, he didn't think he'd ever be able to repay her. Well, he'd just have to see what he could do when she finally contacted him about her travel arrangements.

He gazed across the room, remembering how the morning sun had turned Abby's hair to copper fire, wondering what would compel a woman to give so much of herself to him—a total stranger? She'd gone to great lengths to help him. She'd actually *married* him. He wondered if—

A bubble of baby laughter broke into his thoughts, and his attention returned to his daughter. He smiled, content to simply watch Sona play with her rattle.

Late that afternoon, Ethan and Sona had stopped in the hotel restaurant for some dinner. The menu didn't cater to children at all, so he'd ended up special ordering several different kinds of soft-cooked vegetables and he'd mashed them with his fork. Sona had eaten like a voracious little horse. He'd focused so much of his attention on feeding his little girl, the chicken Kiev and *kasha* he'd ordered for himself had grown stone-cold before he'd taken one bite. But that really didn't matter, especially when he knew his new daughter's belly was full. However, being satiated, Sona had quickly lost interest in the food, the utensils, the napkin, and she had begun to squirm. So Ethan had had to gobble his dinner and quickly find something else to hold her interest. He just chalked it up as being one more thing a new parent must do: eat cold, hasty meals.

Bath time had been an experience. As he had washed from Sona the sticky remains of dinner, she had splashed and squealed with glee. Ethan's shirtfront had ended up as wet as she by the time he'd gotten the soap rinsed off her.

All in all, it had been a long and hectic day. And although he was still experiencing the effects of the adrenaline high caused by his successful adoption, he had to admit he was glad it was time for bed. Because he was dog-tired.

The cot Sona sat on had seemed soft enough, but as soon as it had arrived Ethan had realized that it was much too narrow for Sona to sleep on without the fear of her falling onto the floor in the night. So he'd done his best to barricade all three exposed edges of the mattress. He'd used the pillows off his bed, rolled up his blankets, too. And he'd found an extra pillow in the closet. He studied the soft enclosure he'd created for Sona and sighed. That should keep her safe.

The bare mattress he'd left for himself caught his attention and he couldn't help but grin. Heck, he didn't need a pillow. He could cradle his head on his arm. And he didn't need blankets. The summer night was warm. He doubted that he'd sleep much tonight, anyway, he was so excited. A spontaneous and utterly delighted chuckle rumbled deep in his throat, and the sound had Sona gazing at him with her huge, dark eyes.

She didn't seem half as frightened as she had earlier this afternoon. She handled being with strangers well, and Ethan guessed that had come with her experiences in the orphanage. She probably never knew from day to day who would be caring for her. But he wouldn't be a stranger for long. Each day would bring him and Sona closer. He could feel it in his heart.

Sona tossed the rattle aside and gazed up at him. Then she rubbed her eyes with her tiny fists. Lord, but she was just too cute. She was tired. Any fool could see that.

"It's time to lie down, sweetheart." Speaking softly and approaching her slowly, he picked up the rattle and set it out of reach. Then he eased Sona back until she was lying down in the safe little nest he'd created. Her bottom lip quivered. Her huge, brown eyes welled with the biggest, wettest crocodile tears he'd ever seen in his life.

"It's okay, sweetie," he crooned. "It's time to go to sleep. You're tired. We've had a long day. Daddy's tired, too."

As soon as he'd uttered his new title, a joyous chill coursed across his skin. He was this child's daddy. He picked her up, cradled her head against his shoulder, but her tears continued. Ethan slowly filled his lungs with the soft, baby scent of her.

"Shhh," he said. "Hush, now. It's okay."

"Pisne," she said, her crying making her hard to understand.

"What? You want your rattle?" He picked up the toy and gave it a little shake, but Sona only became more agitated.

She pushed away from him, her weeping developing into hiccuping sobs. Taken off guard by her struggles, Ethan's eyes widened and he dropped the rattle, pressing his hand against her back so she wouldn't slip from his grasp.

"Whoa there," he said. Due to his surprise, his tone was louder than he'd intended.

Sona howled. *"Pisne,"* she repeated over and over between her sobs.

He placed her on the cot, and that calmed her. But only a little. She seemed to be expectant, waiting.

Soon, her tears continued to flow. And Ethan felt suddenly inept.

Her distress magnified. She obviously wanted *something*.

"You're thirsty?" He ran to the bathroom where he'd placed a bottle filled with juice in the ice-packed bucket to keep it cold. "Here, sweetie." He offered her the bottle, only to have her slap it away.

Again, she repeated the word he didn't understand.

Okay, she didn't want her toys. She didn't want a drink.

An idea came to him…maybe she was too warm. Immediately, he reached down and removed the fluffy pink knitted booties he'd bought her this afternoon.

Still, she cried.

He checked her diaper and found it dry.

Her sobs rang like loud, grating bells in his ears. Ethan paused, rubbed the back of his neck, raked his fingers though his hair, his feeling of incompetence swelling with each passing moment.

It wasn't as if he'd thought becoming a parent was going to be easy. He'd known the responsibilities of raising a child would be immense. Even before he'd left America, he'd spent hour upon hour planning what he could do for this little girl when they finally became a family.

He'd clothe her, see that she ate a well-balanced diet. He'd care for her when she was sick. He'd laugh with her when she was happy. He'd teach her games. Catch lightning bugs on hot summer nights. He'd bake peanut butter cookies with her on cool autumn afternoons. They would watch "Sesame Street" to-

gether, learn to count and say the alphabet. He'd hold
the seat of her bicycle, run alongside her, as she
learned to ride. And when she got old enough, he'd
send her to the best private schools. He'd see that
she got piano lessons and ballet lessons. He'd make
certain she participated in any activity that interested
her. He'd save money for her college fund.

These were only some of the plans he had made
during the weeks preceding the adoption. But standing here, seeing his little girl sobbing with the want
of...*something*... And him not knowing what it was
she was asking for.

Ethan thought his heart would rip clean in two.
And then panic set in.

He closed his eyes and inhaled deeply, a dense
shadow rolling over him, smothering him like a wet
wool blanket. How could he have ever believed he
could do this? he wondered. How could he have
thought he could even begin to tackle the enormous
responsibility of this small child's life? His heart
raced, but this time it wasn't caused by euphoria or
joy or happiness—it was due to an overwhelming
doubt in his ability to do right by Sona.

When he raised his eyelids, his gaze fell on the
redheaded doll he'd bought for Sona, the doll that
had reminded him so much of...

Abby. Her name whispered through his mind like
a fresh, spring breeze.

Surely, she would be able to help him. She would
know what it was Sona was asking for. She would
be able to help him stop his little girl's tears.

He glanced toward the phone, mentally shaking
his head. He didn't know her number. Didn't even

know if she owned a phone. But he did know her address. He'd picked her up earlier today in a taxi so they could be married.

Checking his watch, he decided it wasn't too awfully late. She would probably be up. *If* she was at home.

Refusing to think anything else but that she'd be there for him, that she'd be willing to help him, he picked up Sona.

"Let's go, honey," he told her softly, knowing full well she couldn't hear him over her crying. "Let's go for a ride."

Abby sat at the table in the small kitchen of her tiny basement apartment. The cheese she nibbled on, along with the delicious and hearty seven-grain bread, was her dinner. She studied the employment advertisements, intently scanning the page for available teaching positions, and every so often she'd absently reach up and fluff her damp hair.

Sharing a bathroom with the two other basement apartments wasn't all that bad. But Abby didn't like to take too much time in the shower, so she only washed her hair every other day. Tonight was one of those evenings.

After swallowing the last bite of cheese, she wiped her hands on a cotton towel and then slowly, meticulously combed her fingers though her long, wavy tresses. She always let her hair air dry. The intense heat from a blow dryer only made the natural waves kink into frizzy curls.

A long sigh issued from her throat. All evening she'd busied herself with the most mundane tasks:

straightening her already-tidy apartment, hand-washing a few underclothes, taking a quick shower, eating her dinner, studying the same page of the newspaper over and over.

Focusing on the ordinary, the routine, was keeping her mind tightly reined. Preventing her thoughts from wandering. To her outrageous behavior of the past couple of days. To her marriage to a man who was a complete stranger. Shaking her head, she realized that wasn't the entire truth. Thoughts of not the actual marriage, but the stranger himself, were what she was avoiding. The devastatingly handsome man with whom she had exchanged wedding vows.

Ethan. Just thinking his name conjured in her mind a clear and vivid image of his chiseled, swarthy features.

She had known that, in marrying her, Ethan Kimball had been using her. But then, she had *offered* herself to be used. She'd wanted to help him. No, she realized, she had wanted to help that little girl. The child with whom she had more in common than she cared to admit.

However, in working together with Ethan to procure the adoption, Abby couldn't help but feel she'd formed a kind of bond with him. It wasn't an idea that was totally ludicrous, was it? There were other reasons besides love that drew people together. And she and Ethan had found one. Little Sona.

Closing her eyes, Abby effortlessly remembered Ethan's intense, dark gaze when he had thanked her for her help. He'd reached out to her. Touched her cheek. And even now, she tilted her head in some vain effort to capture his strong-yet-tender fingers between her jaw and her shoulder. But all she met was empty air.

Her eyelids flew open. A vague, almost shadowy fear churned in her belly. The emotion confused her, had her looking around the room, her gaze wide, wild, as she searched for something with which to busy herself, some mundane task to occupy her, divert her attention.

She got up, took her plate and glass to the sink, washed them, dried them and put them away on the shelf. But the strange foreboding remained in her stomach, making her feel as if she'd eaten, not a delicious dinner of bread and cheese, but a bowl of dry and tasteless clay that had lodged in the pit of her gut in a hard lump.

This was ridiculous. She'd helped an orphan find a home. She'd helped a man adopt a child.

But Ethan had stirred in her some profound emotions—feelings she didn't quite understand. The undercurrent of attraction was clear, she realized. But then any woman would have found the man appealing. However, it was the fearful feeling, the shadowy apprehension that she couldn't fathom. It wasn't like she was afraid of Ethan. No. That wasn't it at all. The feeling came from somewhere inside herself. Somewhere deep inside...

Abby shook the thoughts away, rushing into the modest sitting room and snapping on the radio. It was high time she put all this out of her head.

Ethan Kimball had already moved on. She had better stop dwelling on the incident—on *him*—and do the same.

A knock at her door had Abby automatically perk-

ing up. Rarely did she have visitors. It was probably
Antonetta. The tea bags in her neighbor's cupboard
seldom lasted to the end of the month. But Abby
didn't mind offering her friend a cup of tea. Especially tonight. This evening she could use a diver-
sion.

The toddler's cries could be heard even before
Abby opened the door. The sound made her frown
in confusion, but the sight of Ethan and Sona on her
threshold made her lips part in utter surprise.

"What's wrong?" she asked, as she tugged on his
sleeve to get him inside. "What happened? Is she
hurt?"

Ethan's deep mahogany eyes were wide with
panic. He shook his head. "She's not hurt. But she's
upset. She wants something. Kept saying it. Over and
over. I couldn't understand. She's been crying. And
asking. For something."

"What?" Abby asked above Sona tearful sobs.
"What was she saying?"

Again his dark head shook. "Dunno. Peez-
something." His frustration mounted.

Abby soothed her hand down the toddler's leg.
"Okay, baby doll, tell Abby what you want."

Sona screeched, hiding her face in Ethan's neck.

"Lord, help me." His whispered prayer was ac-
companied with a quick glance heavenward.
"Honey," he crooned to Sona, "it's okay. Everything is okay."

But the tension in his voice, in every muscle of
his body, conveyed a far different circumstance to
Abby.

Ethan's gaze was pleading when he looked her. *Help me,* it silently asked.

Touching Sona, or trying to take the child from Ethan would only make matters worse, Abby knew. She decided that even addressing Sona when the child was so upset was the wrong course of action. So Abby decided to focus her attention on Ethan. If she could get him to calm down, then maybe Sona would as well.

"Sit down," Abby quietly told Ethan, pointing to an old, worn easy chair.

"I can't," he said.

He jostled the toddler, evidently hoping to rock her into a calmer state. Abby sensed that the anxiety he was feeling was keeping him from realizing just how vigorously he was jiggling Sona.

"You *can*—" she took him by the sleeve of his shirt and directed him closer to the chair "—and you *will.*"

He sat and the jostling stopped. But Sona's tears did not.

"What do I do?" he asked. "Tell me how to make her stop. She's been crying for nearly thirty minutes. She's going to make herself sick."

"She looks so tired," Abby observed.

"We're both exhausted."

He had faint circles under his eyes and his jaw was shadowed with the day's growth of beard. Abby couldn't help but remember how clean and smooth his face had been that morning when they had stood together and...

Stop, she silently chided.

"I'm afraid I might have made a mistake."

His voice held enough doubt and insecurity to melt Abby's heart. Crouching by the chair, she reached out and stroked his arm lightly, taking care not to touch Sona.

"All I wanted was to give her a good life," he continued, miserably. "To make her happy. But how can I do that when I can't even tell what it is she wants?"

"You're going to be just fine," she told him. "You can't have expected every minute to be sunshine and roses. Especially at first. She's got to get used to you."

"But we did just fine this afternoon."

The three of them sat for a moment, Ethan seeking solace from Abby, Abby trying to silently comfort him and Sona, who was releasing distressful, hiccuping sobs.

Then the little girl did the most extraordinary thing. She pressed her tiny palm to Ethan's face and looked him directly in the eye. For a split second the room was filled with an utter and profound silence.

"*Pisne.*" Sona's voice sounded thick from her tearful spell.

Ethan's gaze flew to Abby. "There," he said. "That's it. What does she want?"

Abby smiled. "She's asking for songs. She wants you to sing to her. Whoever put her to bed at the orphanage must have sung the children to sleep."

"Sing?" A crease marred his forehead. "I can't sing."

"Sure you can," Abby encouraged him. "You must remember some simple songs from your childhood."

Ethan shook his head, his frown deepening.

"How about the alphabet song?" she suggested. "Everyone knows that. Surely that's how you learned your letters."

He looked skeptical, but he began to sing the alphabet, his voice tentative, low, but velvety rich. Sona quieted down, sniffed back a hiccup or two and then cuddled up against his chest, plunking her thumb into her mouth.

The sight of this tall, muscular man cradling his tiny little girl in his arms, singing to her softly, made a lump of emotion swell in Abby's throat. It was beautiful. Loving. Serene.

She hadn't expected to see Ethan ever again. What contact she'd anticipated would have been over the phone or through the mail once he'd returned to America. But here he was. In all his broad-shouldered, gorgeous glory. It was enough to make Abby's heart flutter hard in her chest.

Before he'd finished a second repeated verse of the song, his daughter had fallen into a deep sleep. Ethan finished the words, obviously unable to tear his gaze from Sona's peaceful face. Finally, he sighed. The immense relief expelled in that huge exhalation was clearly evident to Abby. They sat for several moments in silence, both of them listening to Sona's steady, even breathing.

His deep-brown eyes were as intent and fixed on Abby as they had been earlier that afternoon just before she'd told him goodbye. Abby suppressed the shudder that coursed deliciously up her spine.

Finally, Ethan whispered, "Thank you. *Again.*"

She was frantic to somehow lighten the mood.

With that idea at the forefront of her thoughts, she cocked up one corner of her mouth into a lopsided grin. "Anytime," she quipped.

The seriousness in his expression didn't soften one iota. "Don't make light of this. If you hadn't been here to help me, to tell me what it was she needed, to figure out she was used to being sung to sleep—" he shook his head "—I don't know what I'd have done."

Softly, she tapped her fingers against his forearm. "It was nothing—"

"Don't."

Sona stirred, and both Ethan and Abby grew stone-still. His intense eyes never left Abby's, and in the end she became discomfited enough that she was forced to break their visual contact by averting her gaze.

Finally, she lifted her face to his, surrendering to his solemn mood. "Okay. You're very welcome."

He didn't respond, simply continued to study her.

She felt the urge to squirm, but she didn't. Instead, she said, "You would have been fine, you know. You'd have figured it out. In time."

His thoughts where churning; she could see it in his expression. Her words seemed to spark an idea in him.

"In time," he murmured. Then he fell silent.

He pondered something, and she couldn't help but wonder what was going on in his head.

"Yes," she said. "You'll—"

"I *will*," he interrupted her. "I'm sure I'll get it right. In time."

She smiled. She liked his confidence. Found it...very enticing.

The observation stopped Abby midthought. Her smile faded. She had to stop this. The best thing to do, she swiftly decided, was to simply ignore the silly attraction she felt for this man.

"Good," she told him, hoping that her tone didn't reveal the ridiculous allure she was determined to suppress. "I'm glad you're seeing things my way."

"But," he continued, "until that time comes, I'm going to need your help."

"Excuse me?"

"I want you to come to work for me. I want you to fly home with me and Sona tomorrow. I want you to be there to help me understand Sona. I want you to teach her to understand me. Teach her to understand English, I mean."

Abby frowned. "Ethan you don't need me for that. Sona is just a baby. Toddlers are like little sponges. She'll soak up English in no time." Her insides began to quake at his startling request. "No time at all."

"You don't have a job," he continued to argue his point. "Let me provide you with one. You can be Sona's nanny. Her governess. Her teacher. *My* teacher. Call yourself anything you want. But come to work for me. We need you."

Her heart lurched in her chest and her mouth went dry.

No, Abby, a tiny voice said. *Don't even consider this.*

There was nothing for her in the United States.

Nothing at all. That's why she'd spent all her time in Europe since graduating from college.

"You don't even know me," she pointed out.

"I know enough," he said. "I know you're the kind of woman who put her whole life aside for two days in order to make a total stranger's dreams come true. You're a good person. Honest. True to your word. That's enough for me at the moment."

"B-but—"

"Abby..."

The quiet desperation in his voice, in his gaze, sliced through the very words she was about to utter.

"...I *need* you."

Chapter Four

His plea was like a physical caress, and Abby went utterly still as she waited for his words to brush warmly against her cheek. She knew very well that it was a silly thought. But still she remained motionless, waiting. Just waiting.

And while she was in that expectant and placid place her thoughts turned to chaos.

There is nothing for you in America. Nothing. That's why—

But Ethan will be there. And Sona. And they need you.

You can not get involved in this. You can't afford to travel to the States. You can't afford it monetarily. Or emotionally.

Frowning, Abby didn't fully understand the implications of the unexpected, dark and whispery notion, but before she could indulge in further examination, other ideas pushed the shadowy concept aside.

But look at him, her brain whirled on. *He loves this child. He wants this little girl to accept him. Wants the two of them to become a family. How can you not help him?*

Easily, another more cynical thought crowded in. *Just say no. Do not allow yourself to become embroiled—*

But they need *you.*

At that moment, Sona stirred. And Abby watched with rapt attention as Ethan automatically lifted his big, strong hand, smoothed his flattened palm ever so gently, ever so lovingly down his little girl's back, comforting her, lulling her into feeling safe and secure.

Never in Abby's life had she met a man who showed more tenderness, more unconditional love. Never had there been a man more worthy of having his most desired wish come true...that of becoming a daddy.

Like the wings of a tiny hummingbird, Abby's heart fluttered against her ribs. She was stunned to realize that the attraction she'd felt for Ethan—the fascination she'd thought she'd successfully repressed—once again reared up out of hiding like a hungry cobra, threatening to swallow her whole. And on the heels of the allure came that same vague fear she'd experienced before, too. A sort of dread that was both obscure and confusing. She swallowed, frantically shoving the puzzling emotions from her.

No. No, she determined with silent force. This *wasn't* attraction she was feeling. This weak-in-the-

knees emotion had to do with the connection she felt
to Sona. The common bond they shared.

It was a flimsy lie, at best. But Abby was in the
perfect mind-set to grasp a tight hold on the thin half
truth.

Sona had the chance of a lifetime here, the silent
voice in Abby's head continued to argue stubbornly.
This little girl could have a family. A father who
wanted her. Who loved her. Cared for her.

And Abby could, once again, have a hand in making that happen.

For Sona, the two small words echoed across her
mind. Then, nodding, Abby looked Ethan in the eye
and said, "Okay. I'll do it. I'll go back to America
with you."

The Philadelphia airport was crowded as Ethan,
Sona and Abby made their way to luggage pickup.
The three of them had ended up staying in Kyrcznovia for another day so Abby could pack up her
belongings, close out her meager bank account and
generally get her life in order.

"I'm a born traveler," she'd told Ethan. "As a
kid, I never stayed in one place for very long. And
my teaching has taken me all over Europe."

Bogging herself down with lots of possessions just
wasn't practical with her constantly-on-the-move
lifestyle. The few bulky items she couldn't pack, she
gave to her neighbor, Antonetta, who was happy to
have them.

"I'm amazed that you've stowed your whole life
into two canvas duffel bags," he'd observed.

She'd pointed out, "And a backpack."

He had chuckled, shaken his head and murmured something about never having met anyone quite like her. Well, that was okay, Abby remembered thinking at the time, because she had never met anyone quite like Ethan, either.

He'd entertained Sona through their long flight. He'd played patty-cake, peekaboo and about a dozen other silly games he'd made up on the spur of the moment. When Sona had finally grown tired, Ethan had sung to her softly, nonsensical tunes that had neighboring passengers casting him odd glances, but the songs had only made Abby smile endearingly.

There seemed to be a new boldness in Ethan since Abby had agreed to return to the States with him. Almost as if he'd had the intent and determination to be a good father to Sona, but with Abby by his side to help him smooth over the rough patches of his initial journey into parenthood, he now had the confidence he needed to really and truly reach his desired destination.

The realization that she had helped to instill some faith in himself made her feel really good. Kind of warm inside. Encouraging people, making them feel capable was part of her job as a teacher. She'd found that motivating her students with positive feedback and doing what she could to bolster their self-confidence only made them more excited about learning. Encouraging Ethan had been easy. It was so obvious that he loved Sona and wanted to be the best daddy he could be.

However, Abby didn't want Ethan to become too dependent on her. So she had been very clear that

she couldn't remain in America for very long. A
month or so, two at the very most.

"Four to eight weeks," Ethan had mused. "I think
Miss Sona and I can get comfortable with one another between now and then."

At luggage pickup, Ethan handed Abby his sleeping daughter so he could gather together their bags.
And soon they were in a hired limo, headed for his
home in the suburbs.

"You work in Philadelphia?" she asked him, realizing that she knew very little about the man she'd
married.

"Actually, I work from home, not too far outside
the city."

The western-most portion of the sky had turned a
dozen different shades of vermilion as the hazy sun
set low on the horizon.

"I design custom computer systems for various
businesses," he added. "Technology is changing
every day. Keeping up with those changes keeps me
in high demand. I've created and updated systems
for companies all over the U.S. I plan to break into
the foreign market soon."

"Sounds like you're off traveling a lot," she commented.

"Nah," he said, shaking his head. "With the In-
ternet, computer E-mail and document attachment
capabilities, fax machines and the good old telephone, I don't usually have to leave my office. Technology's great. And my newest gadget is a video
camera that's hooked up to my computer monitor. I
can attend conference meetings with clients without
getting out of my chair. Of course, once in a while

emergencies arise and I'm forced to travel. But those are rare occasions.''

''I see.''

''With my office right in my home,'' he said, ''I have the perfect setup to be a stay-at-home, work-at-home dad.''

He smiled, his white teeth glinting in the fading twilight, and his handsome face made Abby's breath catch. A funny sort of heat began to curl inside her, low down, deep at her very core.

She glanced out the window at the passing scenery, taking a moment to quell the tendrils of desire that had sprouted to life.

Tossing him a grin, she quipped, ''Stay-at-home, work-at-home dad, eh? I think you may have coined a brand-new phrase for the new millennium.''

Ethan chuckled, and the rich sound vibrated in the quiet confines of the luxurious limousine. Abby felt apprehension begin to twist and spiral through her once again. Thankfully, Sona chose that moment to awaken.

The toddler opened her beautiful dark eyes, blinked awake, and sighed. She immediately struggled to a sitting position on Ethan's lap.

''Well, look who's up.'' Ethan smoothed Sona's bangs from her face. ''Your nap was so long, sweetie, I'm afraid you won't sleep a wink tonight.''

Abby was grateful that his attention was focused on Sona. She desperately needed a moment or two to toss some cold water on the heated desire plaguing her.

''That's okay, though,'' he continued, talking to

his daughter. "We'll get into a routine soon enough."

The tenderness that tinged his voice as he spoke to Sona caused something to happen to Abby. Unexpected tears prickled her eyelids, and she quickly turned her head and stared out the window. What on earth was wrong with her? First, she was forced to tamp down her growing attraction, and now the mere sound of his voice was causing her to well up with emotion.

She was tired from the long day of traveling. That's all it was.

The driver turned down a narrow, winding asphalt lane.

"We're here," Ethan said. "Look, Sona. We're home."

Covertly dashing the heel of her hand against her moist eyes, Abby etched a smile onto her mouth and took a slow, deep, steeling sigh. She was tired, she silently repeated the excuse, and the fatigue was getting the best of her.

His home was a beautiful brick colonial set so far back from the road that she couldn't see or hear the sparse traffic going by. In the ever-dimming twilight, she spied the outline of a building not too far away.

"Neighbors?" she asked.

He shifted Sona on his hip, directing the driver to leave the luggage on the porch by the door and then he gazed out to where she'd been looking. "No," he told her. "That's my barn. I keep two horses. My property butts up against a state park, so I can ride...if I get up early enough. I don't like to bother the hikers." With his eyes still trained on the barn, he said, "I have a cat around here someplace, too. Chunky doesn't come around unless she's hungry. I hire a man to take care of the animals, and the grounds. That way I'm free to work. Bob comes every day. If it hadn't been for him, I wouldn't have been able to stay in Kyrcznovia all that time. I'm sure he took good care of my animals."

Two horses, Abby mused, silently realizing that the property must be substantial. And being adjoined to a park would only increase the value of Ethan's land. The limo he'd hired, with its soft leather seats and silent driver, had been the most opulent vehicle she'd ever ridden in. His business must be very successful in order for him to afford all this just thirty minutes outside a sizeable city, she thought, looking around her.

Ethan looked over the front lawn as the car pulled away down the lane. "The grass looks good. I knew I could count on Bob to take care of the place while I was gone." He reached for one of her duffel bags. "You want to carry Sona? Or some of the bags?"

She smiled, even though she doubted he could see her in the dusky night. "I'll take Sona and one bag. And please don't make it the one I overpacked."

He let them into the house and headed right up the stairs toward the bedrooms.

"You'll have the room at the end of the hallway," he told her.

"The important thing is," she said, "which room will Sona have?"

"Ah..." Ethan set down the bags he was lugging. "Right in here." He pointed. "The room has been ready and waiting for weeks and weeks."

The bedroom was just as cute as it could be, decorated in Mother Goose characters. Humpty Dumpty sat on a wall and Little Miss Muffet was there along with the happy-faced spider who hoped to share her curds and whey. Little Boy Blue was blowing his horn. And the Little Old Lady who lived in a shoe was tending her multitude of children.

Plush blue carpeting covered the floor and the furniture was white. The window coverings were pink. A small toy chest sat in one corner. Ethan had designed the perfect child's room for his little girl, and Abby was quick to tell him so.

"I can't take the credit," he admitted, taking Sona from Abby and setting her down. "I had a decorator come in and do most of the work. But I did pick out the toys. I had a ball in the toy department."

Sona made a beeline for the rocking chair, and with one touch she set it into gentle motion. She looked startled by the movement and turned her lovely doe-eyed expression first to Ethan, then Abby.

Both of them smiled at her antics, then they broke out with soft laughter when Sona tried to climb onto the seat of the chair, but the rockers and the simple laws of gravity had her plunking down onto her bottom on the soft carpet. An instant of fear clouded Sona's eyes as she gazed at Ethan.

"You're okay," he told her. "Don't you worry. You'll learn soon enough how to climb up there." Then he went and took her hand. "Let's go show Abby to her room."

Even though the child didn't understand him, she curled her fingers around his. On his way out the door, Ethan picked up the heaviest canvas bag with his free hand, then he led Sona to the end of the hallway.

"You and Sona will be sharing a bath," he told her, indicating one of the doors they passed with a nod of his head.

She grinned. "That won't be a problem. I've shared a bathroom with an entire floor of families." She chuckled. "I've perfected the five-minute shower."

"Well, there'll be no need of that here." He went through the door of her room, set down her bag and flipped on the light. "There's plenty of hot water. Enough even for a long soak in the tub. Every single day, if you like."

The mere thought of a hot bath was so sinfully sensuous that Abby actually groaned. "You have no idea how wonderful that sounds." When she opened her eyes, she thought she saw a fleeting sense of tension in Ethan's jaw. However, on second glance she didn't see a trace of strain.

She looked around at the pale-green and rich cream decor. "Nice," she told him. "Very nice."

"I hope you'll be comfortable."

The tautness in his voice made Abby frown. Her gaze flew to his face. But he'd dipped his head, busying himself by picking up Sona and smoothing her little dress.

What had she done, what had she said, to cause the change in him? To induce the sudden awkwardness she felt in the air?

"I'm sure I'll be fine." Her assurance sounded vague and far-off.

Ethan walked to the door. "You get yourself settled. I'll take Sona down to the kitchen and see if I can rustle up something for us to eat. There won't be much in the fridge. I've been gone quite a while. It'll probably be soup and crackers.''

''I don't mind cooking—''

''No,'' he cut her off firmly, not bothering to turn back. ''Come on down after you've unpacked some of your things.''

And then he was gone.

Confusion swirled around her along with the cool draft that poured into the room from the air-conditioning vent. Why had things turned so tense? she wondered again.

Finally, she sighed. Maybe she was imagining it. Ethan was surely just as tired as she. Maybe the long hours of travel were catching up to him, too.

She set her backpack on the soft cream-colored bedspread. The carpet and walls of the room were the exact same shade of soft green. The curtains matched the bed coverlet.

Calmness. Serenity. That's what she felt just standing in the middle of the room.

Abby guessed that Ethan had had the room professionally decorated, just as he'd had Sona's. The understated elegance was very nice, indeed.

From the backpack she pulled out her hairbrush and comb and placed them on the dresser. She glanced up into the mirror. The hours of getting from Kyrcznovia to America had taken their toll on her. Her mascara was smeared, her hair, a mess. Rather than unpack her clothes, she opted to go into the bathroom and freshen up a bit. She'd never been a vain person so she didn't fully understand this sud-

den urge to look nice. However, she couldn't help
but suspect it had something to do with the man waiting for her downstairs.

Abby went down the steps, following her nose toward the kitchen. She'd washed her face, brushed her
teeth and run a comb through her hair. She'd applied
a touch of fresh mascara. The short time she'd spent
in the bathroom made her feel like a new woman.

Upon entering the kitchen, her attention was immediately captured by the broad expanse of Ethan's
back. His shoulder muscles flexed and relaxed as he
worked over a skillet at the stove. The small movement was mesmerizing. Abby's pulse raced. She
forced herself to breathe slowly, evenly. Then she
closed her eyelids, overpowering the hypnotic stupor
she'd fallen into.

She was desperate to have something else on
which to concentrate. The kitchen gleamed with
white cabinets and chrome appliances. It was a large,
farmhouse-style room, wide-open and spacious. Finally, when her heartbeat had slowed to a more normal rate, she proceeded further into the room.

"Omelettes." She smiled as she watched Ethan
scooping the fluffy eggs from the pan.

"Yes," he told her. "There was no soup on the
shelves. I hope you like eggs. It's about all we have.
I'll have to go to the store tomorrow."

"I'm so hungry, I'd eat practically anything."
Abby was pleased that he seemed more relaxed than
he had upstairs. His dark mood seemed to have
passed. She was also glad she'd overcome her own
bout with...well, whatever it was that had plagued

her just a moment before. The toaster popped, and she automatically went to pull out the bread slices.

"I found a loaf of bread in the freezer," he told her. "There's butter in the fridge."

While they spent a few more moments preparing the simple meal, Sona concentrated on eating the raisins that Ethan had placed on the tray of her highchair.

"Mmm," Abby commented when they sat at the table together. "This is delicious. Light and fluffy."

"I mix a teaspoon or so of water into the eggs to keep them moist."

"And the cheese." She was silent a moment as she marveled at the taste.

"Swiss." He grinned. "Although I had to cut the hard bits off." Then he cocked his head. "You look like you haven't tasted—"

"I haven't," she admitted, only just able to quash the nearly delirious groan hovering on her lips. "For years. The cheese that's most readily available in the backwoods of Europe is made from the milk of sheep. There's some goat's milk cheese. But no Swiss to be had." She took another moment to chew. "This is *so* good."

Ethan laughed. "Gee," he said, "you're pretty easy to please."

Realizing how silly she must look to him, her face flamed. Then she broke out laughing herself. She shrugged and admitted honestly, "I forgot what I'd been missing." She scooped up another bite of omelette. "This really is good." Her mouth closed over the fork.

After the last bit of egg had been consumed, along

with the last crumb of buttered toast, Abby said, "Why don't you let me clean up? I'll watch Sona and you can go have a shower."

He looked at her a moment. "You know, I think I'll take you up on that offer. I'm going to go look in on the horses, see if I can find that cat of mine and then I'll take a shower."

Later, after Sona had been bathed and dressed in her pajamas, the three of them sat on the floor of the toddler's bedroom. They had pulled out the wooden blocks Ethan had bought weeks earlier, and he and Abby stacked towers that Sona delighted in knocking down. Soon, though, Sona sat down and concentrated on making towers of her own, stacking one block atop the other.

"So," Abby said, "now that you have Sona home, do you want to have a party? To introduce her to your family and friends. I'd be happy to help."

"There's no need for a party." He let a block roll off his palm onto the pretty blue carpet. "I have no family. Well, no close family. I was an only child and my parents died in a boating accident eight years ago."

"Oh, Ethan," she breathed. "I'm sorry."

He accepted her condolences with a small nod. "And the friends I have I made through my business. They're scattered all over the country. And we're not close enough to celebrate something as personal as this." He chuckled suddenly. "Besides that, I keep up with most of them through E-mail on the computer."

How lonely he must be, Abby thought. No family. No close personal friends. Not even a girlfriend...a significant other on whom he could depend during this new phase in his life, in whom he could confide his doubts, his fears, his triumphs and joys.

With her mind still churning over his circumstance, she asked, "So there's no one you need to notify about Sona's arrival into your life? Nobody you want to celebrate with?"

Something in her tone had him looking at her, his brow slightly furrowed. "Don't be feeling sorry for me. My life is just as full as I want it to be. I have my work. I have my horses. My cat." He grinned. "And now I have a daughter. My world has expanded quite nicely, if you ask me."

But you need someone, she wanted to say. You need a companion. An adult. A female adult. A wife.

Realizing her own position, the thought immediately narrowed, focused like a sharp ray of light.

A *real* wife. Someone who would be around to help you raise Sona.

Placing herself in the role she was conjuring never entered her head. She was Ethan's wife, yes. But only for the moment. She was a temporary spouse. *Very* temporary. Her footloose life-style wouldn't permit anything else.

However, once their marriage was annulled, he should really try to find a woman who could and would spend her life helping him make a happy home for Sona. That's what would be best. For Sona. And for him.

Abby wanted to tell him all these things. She wanted to discuss the cons of what she saw as the isolation he'd set up for himself. He might think his world was open enough, full enough, but she didn't.

However, she couldn't bring herself to tell him her thoughts. She just didn't know him well enough. Didn't know how he'd react to unsolicited advice. So she'd have to wait awhile. Until she got to know him just a little better.

Hours later, Abby lay awake in her bed, staring up at the ceiling in the dark. Her exhaustion had had her yawning in Sona's room, and Ethan had urged her to go to bed. He expected Sona to be up late, seeing as how she'd taken such a long nap during the trip home.

When Abby pointed out that Ethan must be just as tired as she, and then offered to stay up with Sona, he'd gently rejected the idea. He was Sona's dad now, he'd proudly reminded her. He was the one who had to get used to the long, sleepless nights that all other single fathers must surely be forced to endure.

He actually seemed eager for the experience, Abby realized. So she had gone off to bed. However, once there, she couldn't sleep even though she was bone weary. She tried reading. Tried listening to slow, soft tunes on the radio. But nothing seemed to help. After what felt like at least a couple of hours of tossing and turning, she finally got up and headed toward the door. What she needed, she decided, turning the knob, was a cool drink of water from the kitchen.

Moonlight streamed in through the bathroom window, casting long shadows in the hallway. She saw a form standing at Sona's door and knew it was Ethan.

"Did she finally fall off to sleep?" Abby whispered, the darkness causing her to move closer than usual just so she could make out his face.

He smiled and nodded. "She looks like a little angel in that crib."

Abby remarked, "She *is* a little angel."

"My little angel." He said the words almost to himself, then he focused his intent gaze on Abby. He was quiet, reflective, as he looked at her in the dark stillness for several seconds. Reaching up, he captured her chin in his fingers. "And she's with me all because of you."

His fingers were warm against her skin. Abby's heart pounded. She studied his eyes. Those profound, sable eyes.

She wanted to blink. To look away. But she simply couldn't. She was lost.

"I was in there rocking her," Ethan said softly, his fingertips sliding, like heated velvet, against her flesh, "and it all just came flooding back to me again. I owe you so much. So much, I'll never be able to repay you."

Her gaze left his only long enough to watch the tip of his tongue sneak out to moisten his sexy lips.

"I only wish there was something I could do to let you know how grateful I am."

The silence that followed was so extreme, so penetrating, that Abby was certain she'd never experienced anything like it in her entire life. Something was going to happen, she was sure of it. Something wonderful. Or something terrible. She didn't know which.

The moment seemed to hover on the very edge of time, and she couldn't decide if the cadence was quickening...or slowing. All she knew for certain was that she was trapped, hypnotized, unable to speak, unable to move, as she waited for the something that was most surely coming.

Then he moved. Not away from her, but *toward* her. And all Abby could do was close her eyes and hold her breath.

Chapter Five

Searing heat. That was the one and only sensation of which Abby was aware when his mouth closed over hers so possessively. Surely her lips would be blistered by his. White-hot, like the burning sands of some distant desert.

Then, slowly, other perceptions seeped into her hazy thoughts. The soft moisture of his kiss tempering the blazing fire. The silken feel of his tongue toying languidly across her lips. When she didn't immediately bid him entry, he lightly, erotically nipped at her bottom lip with his teeth, and it was this nibbling that had her emitting a soft but audible groan.

Almost of their own volition, her arms reached up and slid around his neck. Her fingers entwined themselves in the short, downy hair at the back of his head, pulling him closer. His kiss became more ardent, more demanding, and she opened herself to him, parted her lips so he could venture inside the tender recesses of her mouth.

The desire that shot through her was so pure, so stunningly unadulterated, she was certain she would be scorched to the very soul. She clung to him for dear life, her knees having grown weak and wobbly, and the scant distance she traveled in leaning closer to him changed everything. Heightened the sensations she was experiencing. Snuffing out all her thought processes. Until all she could do was *feel*.

His rock-hard thighs against hers. The solid mass of his chest pressed tight against her breasts. His hands on her face and the small of her back. The heat of his body penetrating her clothing. She breathed in his sweet breath. And he breathed in hers. Again she moaned against his mouth.

Ethan spoke. Some breathless, whispery proclamation that roused her, nudged her out of her passionate stupor, but not soon enough to have heard him clearly.

What had he said? she wondered. Had he murmured a curse? Whispered her name? What?

She blinked, and then realized that he'd pulled away from her several inches. He stared at her, shadows cast across his features obscuring his expression.

Giving a dry swallow, the little hairs on the back of her neck rose as she was thunderstruck with a fear so sudden, so intense that she was barely able to suppress her startled cry. She shoved herself away from him, confused and filled to the brim with this vague and terrible dread.

"I'm sorry," he said.

She only looked at him with what she knew were

huge, panicky eyes, feeling like a wild animal that had been cornered by a vicious hunter. She must escape. She must flee.

"Abby..." he began softly.

For some unknown reason, the regret she heard in his voice only seemed to magnify the panic whirling inside her. Before he could speak—she *must not* give him the opportunity to say another word—she turned on her heel, rushed blindly into her room and shut the door.

The horse's muzzle was like velvet. Abby ran her fingers lightly down the coal-black nose, whispering a soft hello to the animal.

She'd been standing at the stall, intending only to take a quick peek at Ethan's horses before going inside to make the morning coffee. However, while standing there, her thoughts had become sidetracked. She'd tarried so long the horse in the stall had approached her, rubbing the side of its face against the slatted gate, wanting—Abby guessed—a little petting.

"What a pretty boy," she said.

The animal's coat was black as jet, glistening in the morning sunlight that streamed in through the large double doors of the barn. His shoulders were massive, his mane quite thick. And the horse's tail was so long it nearly brushed its back hooves. When the horse had first approached her, Abby had felt hesitant. But it had nickered a greeting and was content when she began to cuddle him a little. Now feeling comfortable with her company, she let her mind continue to wander.

How on earth had she and Ethan ended up kissing last night? That was the very last thing she'd expected...no, that wasn't true. At the very final moment, she'd known something had been about to occur. But a kiss? That had been the last thing she had *wanted* to happen.

But since it had, why had she panicked the way she had? Why had she felt so...filled with fear?

It wasn't as if she'd never been kissed. She was twenty-six, for goodness sake. She'd had dates with men. Not a great deal of them, granted. But she'd had some. And she'd had her share of good-night kisses, too.

So why the overwhelming anxiety?

Thinking about it only made her head ache. The fear that had walloped her last night really didn't matter, she silently concluded, pushing the disturbing thoughts away. What mattered was that she *had* to keep her relationship with Ethan platonic. Europe was her future. She had classes to teach, children to instruct. She simply couldn't get involved.... She shook her head at the unfinished thought.

She'd have to tell him, she decided. She'd have to go over the ground rules they had laid out when she had agreed to travel home with him and become Sona's nanny. She'd have to make her intentions crystal clear.

"Morning."

Abby started, turning to see Ethan standing in the doorway, the bright morning sun behind him. He came forward and the horse nodded its head in obvious excitement. Abby backed a half step away from the stall.

"Hello," she said, the air in the high-ceilinged building feeling suddenly too close.

Ethan handed her one of the mugs of steaming coffee he carried. Then he watched her inhale the rich aroma. She looked beautiful in the morning light with the sun turning her hair to flaming copper. Something deep in his gut stirred, but he clamped a tight, controlling lid on it.

He knew what was vexing him. Desire. He'd felt it early on last night when she'd groaned so deliciously in response to him telling her she could take a nice, long bath. That groan had done something to him. Had provoked a hunger that had threatened to consume him. He'd fought the need, pushed it back. But in doing so, he'd ended up acting short-tempered toward Abby. He was certain she'd noticed it.

And then there had been that kiss.

The kiss they had shared last night should never have happened, he reminded himself for what felt like the thousandth time. Nothing good could come out of it. For her. Or for him. He'd come out here to apologize. To promise that his behavior last night would not be repeated. And with the way she'd run from him last night, he was sure she'd be happy and relieved to hear all the things he intended to say to her.

"Thanks," she told him. And then she took a little sip, her milky-white throat convulsing delicately as she swallowed. The light, flowery fragrance of her skin rose up in his mind. Ethan blinked, quickly focusing his gaze and attention elsewhere.

"I see you've met Pepper."

"So that's his name," she said.

Ethan nodded. "Yeah, he came with the name when I bought him. He's a Morgan."

She frowned.

"Morgan is a breed," he told her, reaching out and running his palm down Pepper's powerful neck. "Originated in Massachusetts, actually. They're pretty easy to spot with their short, broad heads and thick necks. I felt that even though he's pretty independent, he's docile enough to make a good riding horse."

"So, he's mild-mannered, huh?"

Ethan smiled. "With a name like Pepper, you might not think so. But he's pretty complying."

"He's beautiful."

Not as beautiful as you. The thought whispered through his brain, and he swore silently.

He'd told himself over and over last night as he'd tossed and turned that it was completely normal for him to feel physically attracted to Abby. She was a gorgeous redhead. A man would have to be stone-cold dead in his grave not to think her beautiful. However, he refused to ruin his arrangement with her. She'd made it clear she wouldn't be staying around. And that fit his purposes just fine.

But even if she hadn't stated clearly in no uncertain terms that she had every intention of returning overseas, he still wouldn't want to grow too close to her. He liked her too much. Thought she was too nice a person to have her life messed up with his emotional baggage—

"How about this big fellow?"

Abby's question jerked Ethan to attention. He saw that she'd crossed the barn floor to the opposite horse stall. She clicked her tongue, calling Blaze to her, but the horse remained standing at the far wall.

"Blaze can be a little shy," he said. "He'll do better once he gets to know you."

The silence that followed, along with his quick glance at her tight expression, made Ethan aware that she was feeling just as awkward as he.

Evidently noticing the difference in the two horses' builds, she asked, "What breed is he?"

"Quarter horse. The name comes from a quality test established by the original Virginian breeders and had to do with the horses' ability to race a quarter of a mile."

For a few cumbersome seconds, she looked as though she was at a loss for something to say. Finally, she commented, "You know a great deal about your animals."

He shook his head. "Not all that much. I do know they're beautiful and graceful creatures." He offered her a stiff, lopsided smile. "That's enough for me."

Another stilted silence followed. They sipped their coffee, but it was clearly evident that they were both feeling the strain of the drawn-out quiet.

"Sona's sleeping?"

"Yes," he said, eagerly jumping at this change of subject. And then he placed his hand on the intercom attached to his belt. "I can be up in her room in a moment's notice. Lickety-split."

She smiled at the comment he had hoped would thaw the chilly atmosphere between them. He knew what needed to be done. What needed to be said. And he had no idea what he was waiting for.

"Abby, listen," he began, hesitancy making his

voice catch. He gave a little cough and tried again. "About last night."

She stiffened, her gaze automatically dipping to the hay-strewn floor.

"I don't know what got into me," he told her. "It was all my fault. And I apologize. I want you to know that…that kind of thing won't happen again. I need you. And Sona needs you. I was crazy to…do what I did. Wrecking our arrangement is the very last thing I want to do. So I hope you'll accept my apology. And my promise that it won't happen again."

When she didn't immediately respond, Ethan felt that maybe she was looking for explanations along with his regrets and promises.

"I, ah…" he stammered. "All I can say is that it was late. And we'd spent all day traveling. And then I was up with Sona. I was tired."

Her gaze flew to his. "We were *both* tired."

The contrition in her tone took him aback.

"You have nothing to apologize for," he told her. "I was the one at fault. I take full responsibility. And I'm sorry. Terribly sorry."

"B-but…like you said, it isn't going to happen again."

He nodded, relieved to see that she was as eager to put this behind them as he. "You have my word on it."

She smiled then, and it was as if the morning sun had just broken over the horizon.

Sounds of Sona stirring came from the intercom unit hooked to his belt.

"Looks like my little girl is up," he said. "I'd better go fetch her out of bed."

"I guess I could fix us some toast—" after a moment's hesitation, she grinned broadly "—but I have to admit, I'd much rather come and help get Sona dressed for the day. I *am* supposed to be the nanny, you know. I should do something to earn my keep."

Relief flooded through him when he realized that his apology had so thoroughly cleared the awkwardness from the air. Seemed their relationship was back on the right track.

"You'll be doing plenty," he assured her. "I've got a feeling Sona's going to be wanting to know a thousand different things about her new home. I'm just glad you'll be around to help me introduce her to everything."

They headed toward the house, side by side, an apparent, almost lighthearted spring in both their steps.

The days of that first week slipped into a laid-back routine. Ethan worked odd hours in order to spend most of his time with his new daughter. He'd boot up his computer before the sun rose and work several hours before Sona even awoke. When the toddler went down for a nap, he'd head once again to his office. Or if he had work that needed his immediate attention, he'd place Sona on the floor of his office to play with a pile of colorful blocks or other toys.

During the times when he simply had to work, Abby offered time and again to take Sona outside so he wouldn't be disturbed. But Ethan had declined. His reasoning had been that his daughter had to get used to the idea that her new dad was a work-at-home father. If he allowed Abby to care for Sona now, what would he do once she had flown back overseas? No, he'd said, it was best for Sona to get into the pattern of playing in his office when he needed to be at his computer. And Abby had to agree. Of course, he'd told her, she was more than welcome to join in with Sona's fun on the office carpet, and Abby always did.

She'd met Bob, the groundskeeper. He was a kind, elderly man who arrived every morning to feed and groom the horses, and then he'd cut the grass or spend a bit of time weeding the flower beds. He was always gone before noon.

Abby found over the week that her loneliest time was the hour and a half or so when Sona was napping. Ethan was always busy in his office and Abby was left to her own devices. She'd do a little laundry or take a long walk, read a book or watch a little television.

The friendly atmosphere she and Ethan had developed was great, right were it should be. They laughed together, ate together and played with Sona together, neither of them having to worry about that bothersome complication called attraction.

Not that she found him any less attractive now than she had before he'd kissed her. To say that would be a bold-faced lie. He was handsome and intelligent…and he loved little Sona to distraction. *That,* Abby guessed, was his most appealing trait.

When Ethan chuckled at his little girl's antics, Abby thought a more charming smile, a more delectable laugh, couldn't possibly be found.

Yes, she had to admit that he was *the* most handsome man she'd ever met. And she felt free to acknowledge that to herself now…because of his promise to keep things on a "friends only" basis.

When he'd explained that his kiss had been all due to the fact that he'd been overtired, she remembered admitting they had *both* been overtired, and she felt the desperate need to explain her own eager participation in the passionate event. However, the important thing was that he'd assured her it wouldn't happen again.

He hadn't kissed her because he'd felt attracted to her. For some reason, in knowing that she felt free to admire him from afar, without suffering that confusing and dark anxiety. She delighted in watching him with Sona. Or when he was deep in thought in front of his computer screen while she and Sona played quietly on the carpet. And he was a magnificent horseman, his powerful thighs flexing as he cantered Blaze in the enclosed paddock.

She did feel as if she were a help to him. At fourteen months of age, Sona didn't know all that many words. However, the child did know some. And she was bright and inquisitive and loved to communicate. So Abby was happy that she was able to interpret the few phrases and words that Sona spoke. Soon, she hoped the toddler would begin to speak a little English.

"Hey—"

Ethan's voice had her looking up from the magazine she'd been paging through.

"Sona's up from her nap. How about a trip to the mall? We've been cooped up in this house long enough."

Abby grinned, tossing the magazine aside. "I'd

love it!'' She stood up, instinctively smoothing out the wrinkles of her long skirt. ''I haven't been to a big, glorious American mall in...*years.*''

Sona enjoyed a bottle of chilled apple juice on the drive to the shopping center. When Ethan pulled the car into a parking slot and cut the engine, Abby looked at the huge building and felt a thrill shoot through her. Like many women, she loved to shop. But there was nothing like this in the small, Eastern European countries in which she'd worked for the past five years. Besides that, her meager paychecks allowed for no extravagance whatsoever. Her money was strictly spent on necessities alone: food, rent, clothing...and the only clothes she bought were sturdy items to replace those that had become worn.

Ethan buckled Sona into a state-of-the-art stroller. The child looked about her, seeming to marvel at the contraption.

''Every experience seems so awe-inspiring to her,'' Ethan noted.

Abby nodded. ''A lot of that has to do with her age. Kids are just normally curious. But some of it, I'm sure, comes from the fact that she was probably born into a poor family. Otherwise, she'd have found a home with relatives when her parents died. Sona's probably never ridden in a car. Or any kind of motor vehicle. She's probably never been strapped into a stroller and wheeled around. So all of this stuff is new...''

Ethan grinned. ''It's almost like she's in one big amusement park.''

''Something like that,'' Abby agreed.

They went into the cool confines of the building,

and Abby couldn't suppress the smile that spread across her mouth.

"You can't imagine how wonderful this is," she breathed, gazing around at all the colorful window displays. There was an electronic store selling computers and telephones and tiny, portable radios. Another store sold ladies' fashions. Another, books of every description. Yet another, CDs and cassettes of every imaginable music known to man. And that was only within eyesight of the one small wing where they had entered the building.

Tucking her bottom lip between her teeth, Abby openly gaped at the colorful clothing displayed in the window of the apparel shop.

Ethan's laugh drew her attention.

"You look like a kid with her nose pressed up against the glass in a candy store."

Abby couldn't stop the chuckle that welled up from inside her. "I *am* like a kid in a candy store. You have no idea how different shopping is over there."

She knew he understood she was talking about the countries where she'd lived and worked for the past few years.

"You're right," he said. "I do have no idea. So tell me."

"Well," she began, "the economies of most of the Eastern Block countries where I've been teaching are poor. Goods are hard to come by. Up until just a few years ago, women sewed or knitted their own clothing. Some still do. And with the family income coming in at around two to three hundred dollars a month, there isn't much money for luxury items such as satin nighties or silk blouses. Those kinds of things can't even be found. Sturdy. Durable. That's what people are forced to focus on." She chuckled. "Kind of takes some of the fun out of shopping."

"I can imagine," he said.

"And some very necessary items can be extremely hard to find," she continued. "When I first moved to Kyrcznovia, it took me two full weeks to find a small refrigerator. And that one was secondhand."

"Wow. I had no idea. It makes me feel a little guilty for having so many…things."

"Don't," she told him. "You work hard for your money. Just be grateful for all that you have."

"I'll try to keep that in mind." He absently rocked the stroller back and forth to keep Sona happy.

A particularly gorgeous green silk blouse caught Abby's attention and she sighed. "It's so pretty."

"Let's go in," he suggested. "You can try it on."

"Oh, no." She waved aside the idea. "I can't possibly afford it."

"So?" he said. "When has that ever stopped a woman from trying on pretty clothes?"

Abby had to laugh. Finally, she shrugged, her blood pumping with the anticipation of feeling that silky fabric between her fingertips. "Okay. Let's go." Succumbing to his suggestion only had her feeling decadently evil…in the most fun sort of way.

The blouse was heavenly against her skin. She slid her arms into the short sleeves, and as she fastened the buttons, she glanced in the mirror at herself. The color was so rich. Striking. Clothing dye of this quality simply wasn't available in the back hills of Kyrcznovia. She pulled on the complementary taupe walking shorts, zipped them and fastened the leather belt. Then she stepped out of the fitting room.

"Wow!" Ethan remarked. "You look great."

She flushed at his compliment. "Thanks."

The sales lady offered her another coordinated outfit to try.

"Oh, no," Abby politely declined. "We're just having a little fun."

Ethan's brows raised. "Is there any reason we shouldn't go on having a little fun?" he asked.

He was impossible, she thought. She cocked her head a fraction and tried to stare him down, but he refused to budge.

"Okay," she finally whispered, heaving a sigh of surrender as she took the proffered outfit from the woman.

Four times she went into the fitting room. She tried on two shorts outfits, one paisley dress in turquoise, and a black skirt and royal-blue blouse combination. Ethan raved about each one. And Abby just beamed. She couldn't help it. His appreciation made her feel...feminine. Pretty.

Finally, she came out of the fitting room in her own clothing. "No more," she pronounced firmly.

Ethan just chuckled at her. He turned to the sales lady. "Wrap them up."

"No, Ethan!" Abby was horrified. She hadn't tried the clothes on with any intention of buying them. "This was only for fun. That's what you said."

"And it'll be even more fun if they're yours."

"B-but," she stammered.

"Let me do this for you, Abby," he said softly. "I *want* to."

He handed the woman his credit card to pay for the packages.

Before they left the mall, Ethan had bought himself software for his computer, "a business expense," he'd called it. Sona had a new outfit and a new stuffed dalmatian puppy that she refused to put in a sack but carried the cute animal tucked up under her little arm. And besides the four new outfits, Abby also carried from the mall a new pair of dress shoes.

"They're ridiculously flimsy," she told him when he'd insisted on the purchase. "They'll never hold up in the mountainous winter."

Ethan only shrugged. "But they are fashionable."

And they had both broken out in laughter.

They climbed into Ethan's car, buckled up their seat belts and he said, "How about some dinner? I'm sure Sona must be starved." He looked at Abby. "So what will it be? Indian? Italian? French? This city has anything you could want."

He pulled into traffic, and Abby watched him. Should she ask? she wondered. Would he be upset with her when she told him what she'd *really* like to eat?

"Well," she hesitantly began, "if you really want to know…"

Ethan glanced at her. "I really do," he said.

Still, she hesitated. Finally, she blurted, "I'd like a burger."

"A *hamburger?*" He looked incredulous.

Her brow wrinkled in an apologetic expression and she nodded slowly. Then she confessed further,

"And not just any burger. I want it from a fast-food joint."

His mouth quirked up in a disbelieving smile. "You are kidding, right?"

"Nope." Then she rushed to explain, "I haven't eaten good old, greasy fast food for...I couldn't tell you how long." She placed as much suffering and hardship as she could muster into her tone.

Again, he chuckled. "Okay," he said, finally relenting. "Let's give the poor, deprived lady what she wants."

After the last French fry had been devoured, the last remnants of the milk shakes slurped up through straws, Ethan said, "Well, now I guess everyone can go home happy."

Nodding, Abby told him, "Well, I'm a lady with new clothes, new shoes and belly full of greasy fast food." Leaning back, she smoothed her palm over her belly. "I really don't think I'm in Philadelphia at all."

He balled up the hamburger wrappers, tossing the paper onto the tray. "And where is it you think you are?" he asked Abby, humor feathering the corners of his mouth.

She swiped her lips with the paper napkin one last time, and whispered, "Heaven."

He shook his head ruefully. "You are just too easy to please. That's all there is to it."

Abby felt good. Content, even. She and Ethan and Sona had spent a wonderful afternoon together, shopping, eating, laughing. As they drove toward home, she couldn't help but feel that now would be the perfect time to talk to Ethan about her observations. Tell him what was on her mind.

She really thought he needed to find himself wife. A good woman who could help him make a home for Sona. Someone he could share his life with, be with.

When the idea had first come to her, she simply hadn't thought she knew him well enough to be giving him advice. But a whole week had gone by. A week during which they had spent lots of time together. And after their lovely day, maybe he would be open to a little friendly counsel.

Turning her head, she checked on Sona who was happily chewing on the ear of her new stuffed puppy. Then Abby looked at Ethan's handsome profile, held her breath for the fraction of a second that it took for her to formulate how to broach the topic. No better way, she decided, than to simply come right out with it.

Then she blurted, "You know what you need?" Without giving him a single moment to respond, she dramatically proclaimed, *"A wife."*

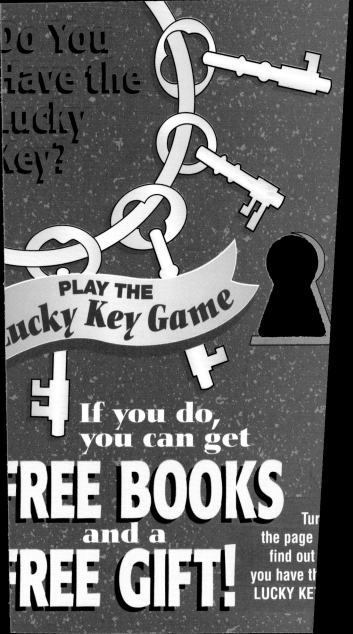

PLAY THE
Lucky Key Game
and ge

HOW TO PLAY:

1. With a coin, carefully scratch off gold area at the right. Then check the claim chart to s what we have for you — **FREE BOOKS** and a **FREE GIFT** — **ALL YOURS FREE!**

2. Send back this card and you'll receive brand-new Silhouette Romance® novels. Thes books have a cover price of $3.50 each in the U.S. and $3.99 each in Canada, but th are yours to keep absolutely free.

3. There's no catch. You're under no obligation to buy anything. We charge nothing — ZERO — for your first shipment. And you don't have to mak any minimum number of purchases — not even one!

4. The fact is thousands of readers enjoy receiving books by mail from the Silhouette Reader Service™ months before they're available in stores. They like the convenience of home delivery and they love our discount prices!

5. We hope that after receiving your free books you'll want t remain a subscriber. But the choice is yours — to conti or cancel, any time at all! So why not take us up on our invitation, with no risk of any kind. You'll be glad you di

YOURS FREE!
A SURPRISE MYSTERY GIFT

We can't tell you what
it is...but we're sure
you'll like it! A
FREE GIFT—
just for playing the
LUCKY KEY game!

FREE GIFTS!

NO COST! NO OBLIGATION TO BUY!
NO PURCHASE NECESSARY!

PLAY THE
Lucky Key Game

Scratch gold area with a coin.
Then check below to see the gifts you get!

YES! I have scratched off the gold area. Please send me the 2 Free
books and gift for which I qualify. I understand I am under no obligation to
purchase any books, as explained on the back and on the opposite page.

315 SDL CYAG   **215 SDL CX97**

Name
(PLEASE PRINT CLEARLY)

Address   Apt.#

City   State/Prov.   Postal Zip/Code

🔑🔑🔑🔑 **2 free books plus a mystery gift**   🔑🔑🔑 **1 free book**

🔑🔑🔑 **2 free books**   🔑 **Try Again!**

The Silhouette Reader Service™ — Here's how it works:

Accepting your 2 free books and gift places you under no obligation to buy anything. You may keep the books and gift and return the shipping statement marked "cancel." If you do not cancel, about a month later we'll send you 6 additional r and bill you just $2.90 each in the U.S., or $3.25 each in Canada, plus 25¢ delivery per book and applicable taxes if an That's the complete price and — compared to cover prices of $3.50 each in the U.S. and $3.99 each in Canada — it's a bargain! You may cancel at any time, but if you choose to continue, every month we'll send you 6 more books, whi may either purchase at the discount price or return to us and cancel your subscription.

*Terms and prices subject to change without notice. Sales tax applicable in N.Y. Canadian residents will be charged applicable provincial taxes and GST.

If offer card is missing write to: Silhouette Reader Service, 3010 Walden Ave., P.O. Box 1867, Buffalo, NY 14240-1867

BUSINESS REPLY MAIL

FIRST-CLASS MAIL   PERMIT NO. 717   BUFFALO, NY

POSTAGE WILL BE PAID BY ADDRESSEE

SILHOUETTE READER SERVICE
3010 WALDEN AVE
PO BOX 1867
BUFFALO NY 14240-9952

NO POSTAGE
NECESSARY
IF MAILED
IN THE
UNITED STATES

Chapter Six

"*What?*" he said.

She had to admit, he looked truly perplexed. He had obviously heard her clearly, but it seemed he had no clue why she'd make such an outlandish suggestion.

"Well, um..." She suddenly felt a little less sure of herself and the advice she was about to offer. Finally, she stammered, "A...a wife. You know. A real wife. A woman who—"

His bewilderment seemed to instantly dissolve. "I have a wife, thank you."

His tone was pleasant enough. Joking, even. And she noted that his mouth was curled up at the corners. A thought came to her. He thought she was teasing him.

"I'm serious, Ethan."

He glanced at her, confusion and wariness returning to his dark eyes. Then he quickly directed his gaze back out at the roadway ahead.

"You lead an awfully solitary life," she said. "It would be good for you—and for Sona—if you had someone with whom you could...share things. I mean, I'm here now. And we laugh at the mischief Sona gets herself into." Abby looked out at the horizon, thinking of their week together. "Like the few moments this week she scared us to death when we couldn't find her. And all the time she was sitting in your closet, playing with your shoes."

Even now, Ethan chuckled easily. "She had lined them all up. She was making a train."

"And when she first met Chunky," Abby reminded him. "She squealed with glee and went toddling after that cat as fast as her tiny legs would carry her."

"And Chunky went running, too," Ethan said. "Poor thing didn't come out from under the porch for hours."

Abby allowed a silence to fall between them. Then she said, "You're going to have a million of those kinds of things happen while Sona's growing up. You should have someone to share them with. It's been nice for me to be that someone. But I won't be here much longer." She felt the need to reiterate. "You'll need someone."

Ethan didn't take his eyes off the highway. "I'll share those times with Sona."

That's not the same thing, she wanted to tell him. She wondered if he was purposefully missing her point.

"You're going to have some rough spots ahead of

you," she pointed out. "When Sona is exposed to other children, she's sure to get chicken pox. And she's bound to come down with bouts of chest colds, and ear infections, once the weather turns chilly. You'll need someone's help. A real, stick-around wife would be the perfect solution."

The light laughter he emitted was forced. "Believe me, Abby, my daughter is the only female I need in my life."

Heck, she'd waded out into the swamp this far, she may as well dive into the deep end.

"I know you told me you were a confirmed bachelor," she began, "but I honestly didn't think you meant...forever. But now I'm getting the feeling that you...have no intention of *ever*...um...getting involved."

He pulled onto the main street that wound through his neighborhood. "I told you that when we first met."

Abby gave a small shrug. "Well, yes. But I kind of thought that might be because you just hadn't met the right woman. Or something."

His lips pursed, and he said nothing.

"However, over the past week I've heard you make...certain comments. Things that have led me to believe you really mean to stay single." She felt the muddy waters closing in around her, but she couldn't help but ask, "Were you hurt in the past?" Then she quickly said, "I mean, you don't have to tell me if you don't want to. But it's awful not to be able to trust. Not all women—"

"Wait," he said, turning the steering wheel and directing the car onto his long driveway.

But Abby was on a roll. "—are evil," she plowed full steam ahead. "You need someone, Ethan. You need a woman who is willing to stay—"

"Are you vying for the position?"

This unexpected question had her spine straightening in surprise. She blinked several times. "Of course not. This isn't about me. How could you think that it is? I can't stay here. You know that. This is about you. And Sona. The two of you need someone to—"

"Stop."

The one small word was quiet, but tight as a coiled spring, and it cut Abby's sentence to the quick.

"You've got it all wrong," he told her. "I wasn't hurt in the past. No one trampled on my feelings. No one damaged my ego. No one wounded my pride."

He put the car in Park, cut the engine and got out of the driver's seat. He opened the back door and unlatched Sona from her car seat. It was clear to Abby that he was simmering with anger, and she wondered how the simple situation had gotten so out of hand.

With Sona on his hip, one of her arms curled around his neck, the other snuggling her new stuffed puppy, he gazed steadily at Abby who remained, stunned to stillness, in the front seat of the car.

"Despite what you might believe, there wasn't some evil woman in my past who destroyed my ability to place my confidence in others." He hoisted Sona into a more secure position in his arms. "I have no trust issues. Believe me. If I did, I wouldn't trust *you* with what has become the absolute treasure of my life."

Then he directed his attention at Sona. "Come on, sweetie. It's time for you to have a nice bath and get ready for bed."

He closed the door of the car and went toward the house, leaving Abby sitting all alone in the total silence.

She watched him disappear into the house. She felt wounded, chagrined, and fully put in her place. All she had meant to do was offer a little friendly advice. Why had her amiable intentions gone so awry?

Let it go, a tiny voice warned from the very back part of her brain. *It's none of your business.*

So he had no trust issues. She nearly nodded when she remembered the confidence in his voice when he made the proclamation. He was telling the truth, she decided. And he'd given her ample proof. If he didn't trust her, he'd never in a million years have allowed her near Sona.

But why…

Let it go, the small voice repeated the command, this time more fiercely.

But Abby only found herself becoming even more curious than she'd been before.

He'd confirmed, once again, his aversion to marriage and relationships. But if his antipathy hadn't been caused by a woman from his past…what *had* happened to bring about this adamant way of thinking? Why was he so tenaciously against marriage? Against loving relationships?

She sat in the silence of the car for a long while, pondering the curious questions flying around in her head like tiny, persistent gnats that simply refused to stop being an annoyance.

* * *

The feminine flowery scent that continuously wafted from Abby filled Ethan's office. It permeated the air, hovered around him, filled his lungs with each and every breath he took.

The two of them hadn't spoken more than simple pleasantries ever since the evening she'd made that odd recommendation to him.

A wife. Abby thought he needed a wife.

He realized she was only making the suggestion because she cared about him and Sona. Abby wanted his little family to thrive once she flew off overseas to her next teaching position. After mulling over the conversation, he eventually understood that her motives were completely unselfish.

His angry knee-jerk reaction had built up a wall between them. A wall they were finding impossible to tear down.

He should apologize for snapping at her as he had. But he just couldn't bring himself to do that. Because then he'd be forced to explain his behavior. And that was simply something he couldn't imagine doing. Walking over red-hot coals was something he'd be more willing to do than to tell Abby the truth about why he never intended to marry.

Darting a covert glance at where Abby and Sona sat on the carpet, he clenched his jaw. Abby was a beautiful woman. With her fiery hair trailing down her back, her jewel-green eyes so inquisitive and lively. Being in the same room with her was torture for him. That's not entirely true, he silently amended. Just *thinking* about her was torture for him. Her luscious curves, her womanly scent…

Stop! he commanded himself. This was insane. If

he kept dwelling on these thoughts of her, he'd never conquer the urge to reach out to her, kiss her, touch her, *taste* her. He held his breath, suppressing a moan of sheer torment. This need was so damned vexing!

"Look, Sona," Abby said softly. "Daddy's watching us draw."

Actually, it was Abby who was doing the sketching, forming big, colorful shapes and then naming them in English for Sona.

The fact that she'd caught him watching her made him feel awkward.

"That's a circle, sweetie," she told Sona. "A big, green circle." Then Abby looked up at him. "That's a hard word to form. *Circle*. But she'll be speaking English very soon."

There it was, he realized. The bright but forced friendliness that was like concrete and bricks. The wall they had erected to protect themselves. Abby's gaze slid from his, telling him she recognized the barrier.

Damn it! He hated this tension. He stared, unseeing, at his computer screen. But how could he ease it without being forced to reveal—

"Ethan."

His gaze flew to Abby's face. Something in her tone had him feeling wary. Her eyes held a hint of sadness.

"I know I told you I'd stay and help you for a couple of months, but maybe it would be best if…"

Her voice faltered, and she took a deep breath.

In a firm tone, she said, "Maybe it's time for me to go. You and Sona are getting on just fine."

And things between us are so awkward, he heard
her silent message.

His whole body tensed. "You can't go yet."

"But..."

"The only reason things have gone so smoothly
is because you've been here to interpret for me."

Abby looked dubious. "You know most of what
Sona says now. She asks for milk. Or cookies. Or
tells you her diaper's wet. Elementary things. Things
you'd figure out even if I wasn't here."

"You can't go yet," he repeated.

Why was he feeling so threatened by her suggestion to leave? His mind was whirling too quickly to
come up with an answer.

Her voice quieted as she said, "The situation between you and Sona might be smooth and sweet
as...as homemade vanilla pudding. But things between you and I..." She hesitated, pressed her lips
together, and then began again. "I keep wondering
when one of us is going to have the guts to admit
that thunderclouds are hovering over us. *Again.*"

Ethan didn't want to discuss the moments right
after their shopping excursion and their fast food dinner a few days ago. He didn't want to have to explain
his behavior, his anger. So he remained silent.

"Look," she told him, "it was never my intention
to bring discord into your home. Don't think I
haven't noticed how little work you've gotten done
since I made that stupid suggestion to you the other
night about your finding a wife."

She was obviously waiting for him to say something. He didn't. *Couldn't.*

"I should have kept my advice to myself," she

said. "I know that now. And I'm sorry that I made you angry." She looked down at Sona and then back at him. "Living with this...silence, this awkwardness is silly. It's time for me to go. You can send the annulment papers to me. I can sign them—"

"The annulment." His eyes went wide.

After only a second's hesitation, she said, "What about it?" Then her head cocked to the side. "You have been working on it, haven't you?"

Oh, heavens. Ethan actually groaned.

"Abby, I forgot all about it."

"You forgot?" Her brow creased as she evidently wondered how such a thing could have happened.

"I'm sorry." He stood up, searching the desk for his book of phone numbers. "I'll call my attorney. Today. I'll get the paperwork started. It can't take long to get the necessary forms filed." With his little black address book in hand, he headed for the door of his office. "You and Sona stay put. I'll use the telephone in the kitchen."

For the life of him he couldn't understand his frantic reaction to her proposal to leave. Even though he knew she'd meant it as an offering—a *peace* offering, he was sure—he hadn't taken it that way at all. But for some reason, he intuitively heard a...threat. And that's what had him feeling the need to escape his office, her. He didn't understand *why* he was feeling threatened...just that he *was*.

At the door, he turned to face her, trying hard to calm his thoughts, get himself under control.

"About the trouble between us," he said. "We'll talk. Okay? We'll smooth things out. We'll make it better. I don't want you to feel uncomfortable around

me. But you can't leave me just yet. Not until Sona
can communicate with me. I...I need you.''

That was as much as he was able to admit before
turning on his heel and escaping.

That night, Ethan was unable to sleep so he went
downstairs and snapped on the television. The news
anchor's voice droned softly in the still room as
Ethan's thoughts churned.

He'd been jumpy and preoccupied all evening.
Sona had sensed his agitation and she'd ended up
acting fussy, refusing to go to bed. In the end, she'd
cried herself to sleep while he'd rocked and sung
until his throat felt raw. That had been the first time
that had happened since they had left Sona's home
country. Abby had hovered around the nursery door.
She'd asked only once if there was anything she
could do. He'd turned down her offer, feeling the
need to handle the problem on his own. Finally,
Abby had gone into her room and shut the door.
Ethan had felt both relieved...and very much alone.

He knew what was wrong. He had to make things
right with Abby.

Their relationship was so darned volatile. Like a
seesaw, they tilted back and forth. They had started
out great. Then he'd made the mistake of kissing her.
And no sooner had they gotten *that* situation worked
out and explained away, when he'd become angry
over her simple suggestion that he marry. Yep, he
silently decided, their friendship was most definitely
like a teetering playground seesaw.

Making peace with her was what he needed to do.
But the problem would be in apologizing without

explaining too much. To go into too much detail about his past would surely make him look bad in her eyes.

At that moment, she rounded the corner. Ethan's breath caught in his throat. She looked like a vision in her simple white nightgown, the thin straps revealing her milky-white shoulders.

"I'm sorry," she said. "I didn't know you were down here."

"It's okay," he told her. Something in her gaze had him asking, "Are you okay?"

"I—I just had a bad dream." Reaching up, she combed her fingers through her long hair. Then she placed her palm at the base of her throat. "I thought I might have heard something outside."

Ethan scooted to the edge of the couch. "I've been down here for a while. I haven't heard a thing."

She still looked uneasy. He stood up.

"Let me go outside and have a look around." The relief and gratitude reflected on her beautiful features made him feel ten feet tall.

The night was still and hot and quiet. He checked the perimeter of the house, the garage and then went into the barn. Both horses were breathing slow and steady, obviously asleep. The only excitement was when Chunky darted from the corner of the barn and curled around his legs looking for some attention.

Bending down on his haunches, Ethan scratched the cat behind the ears. "You out hunting, girl?" he asked. Chunky meowed, her ears pricking up, and then she plunged back into the long shadows cast by the moon.

When Ethan returned to the house, Abby had obviously gone upstairs to fetch her housecoat. The delicate curves of her shoulders were no longer visible, but Ethan knew that all he had to do to if he wanted to conjure them was to close his eyes.

Quickly pushing the thought from his mind, he told her, "All's clear. Everything's quiet out there. Not a sign of trouble."

Appreciation shined in her sparkling green eyes. Ethan looked away, forcing himself to breathe slowly.

"I made us some tea," she said, using a spoon to stir the hot liquid in one mug. "I hope you don't mind having some company for a little while. I sometimes have trouble sleeping. Not often. But sometimes." She gave a slight grimace, her voice softening. "Tonight seems to be one of those times."

The small apologetic smile she gave him made his heart lurch. The thoughts of her and the state of their friendship that had been keeping *him* awake were at the very forefront of his mind.

"Listen, Abby," he said, easing himself down on the couch beside her, "I'm awfully sorry if…if the tension between us is upsetting you to the point that you're losing sleep."

He unwittingly rubbed his fingers across his forehead. "I've been thinking about…you and me. About how our…friendship has been riding some sort of seesaw ever since we met." He swallowed. "One minute we're having great fun together, the next minute I'm…biting your head off."

The memory of the words he'd tossed at her after their shopping trip made him flinch. He murmured, "I'm sorry about that, too." He rushed ahead. "I want us to get along. Sona and I are going to need you for weeks yet. I want you to be comfortable here. I want you to feel at home.''

She laced her fingers around her mug of tea. ''I won't lie to you. It does bother me to know that you're angry with me. I should never have brought up the subject of your marrying—''

''I'm not angry,'' he quickly told her.

Her smile was small as smiles go, but seeing it did strange things to Ethan. His blood seemed to heat up, the muscles low in his gut tightened. Reaching for his mug of tea, he averted his attention from her long enough to get a firm grip on the physical reactions of his body. However the reactions were autonomic; there wasn't much a person could do to control rising blood pressure. Or runaway testosterone.

When he finally did look at her again, he firmly repeated, ''I'm not angry, Abby. Honest.'' Then he said, ''And I'm sorry I snapped at you. I shouldn't have been so...curt.''

Fully intending to let it go at that, Ethan eased back on the couch and stared at the television screen. He simply couldn't explain himself further. He couldn't afford to reveal his past to her. She'd never understand. Hell, he didn't understand how he could have done what he did. How could he expect Abby to? So, he'd simply say nothing more about it.

The quiet grew ever more noticeable with each passing second. Darting a covert glance her way, Ethan saw that she, too, was watching the TV. But there was something about her air, something about the tightness in her shoulders that revealed that she really wasn't as absorbed by the colorful car commercial playing on the screen as she pretended to be.

He felt an...expectation about her. As though she wanted to talk.

Ethan could easily understand that, seeing how nervous she was when she'd first appeared in the living room. He decided it would be in her best interest if he were to engage her thoughts. Get her mind on something else. Make her forget, at least for a while, about the bad dream that had disturbed her.

"You know," he began, "I was raised in this house."

"Oh," she said, lifting her gaze to his, "that's nice. I know I've said this before, but it bears repeating. You do have a beautiful home."

He smiled and accepted her compliment with a small nod. "I was born right here in Philadelphia. Went to grade school here. And college." After a moment's hesitation, he asked, "Where were you born? Where do you call home?"

His smile wavered when he saw her stiffen. She was quick to try to hide her reaction. But not quick enough.

"Well, I was born in Elkhart, Indiana," she told him. "But home is wherever I happen to be."

Was it his imagination, or did she place an extra bit of emphasis on her final statement?

"So you're a midwestern girl, huh?"

Abby only smiled, then busied herself taking a sip of tea.

"What did your dad—"

"I don't have a dad."

She seemed just as surprised by her blurted statement as he was. Color flushed her cheeks with obvious embarrassment.

"Of course I had a father," she corrected. "What I meant to say was that I never knew him, never met him."

Her nervousness was apparent.

"Ah, so you were raised by your mother?"

Abby's gaze slid from his. "No." The tiny word was barely discernable. "I was raised in foster homes."

"Oh," was all Ethan could think of to say, and he'd been helpless to keep his surprise at bay.

Then the most peculiar thing happened. Abby sat up straighter, fixed a bright smile on her face and allowed her usual happy-go-lucky persona to shine through.

"It wasn't a bad life," she told him. "In fact, I'd say, all in all, I had a pretty good childhood. I learned to deal with all different kinds of people by living in all those homes. With all those—"

There was the smallest of hesitations here, but Ethan couldn't help but notice it nonetheless.

"—families. I learned independence. I learned that I can count on myself. That I can be my own best friend." She nodded happily. "I learned I can survive. Just about anything."

The easygoing, upbeat rhetoric seemed somehow...*off*. Something wasn't right. Her positive show was just that. A show. Ethan got the distinct impression that Abby was desperately trying to cover something. And her efforts were nearly successful.

Nearly.

He should back off. He knew that. If she wanted

to hide behind a smile, then he should let her. But there was something about her eyes. A sad light that glistened in her green gaze. A poignant aura needing release. It touched Ethan. Called out to him. And he felt he simply had to reach out. To answer.

"It really wasn't all that wonderful. Was it?"

For a moment, her features hardened into a fierce, protective mask, and he thought she had every intention of remaining hidden behind the wall of blithely optimistic energy she'd erected.

But then his gaze was drawn to a small movement of her creamy throat as it convulsed with a tense swallow. Her shoulders slumped, and the sigh she breathed overflowed with weariness.

Chapter Seven

Her vulnerability was nearly his undoing. He wanted to reach out to her. Touch her. Calm her. Let her know that, no matter what she might have endured, everything was going to be okay. That he'd make it so.

But he battled the overwhelming urge to make physical contact. He knew doing so wouldn't be appropriate. However, he intended to connect with her in other ways. With concern. Kindness. Caring. As much as he was able to, anyway. Because these were the things he sensed she needed now.

"You, um," she finally stammered softly, "you're absolutely right."

Her voice sounded so young, so assailable. His impulse to protect her increased tenfold.

"My childhood wasn't all that wonderful."

The awkwardness in the set of her shoulders, the discomfort in her expression clearly conveyed to him that this hard-wrought admission went completely against the grain of her normal easygoing, affable nature. Ethan recognized at that moment that she hid a great deal behind that gorgeous smile of hers and his curiosity kicked into high gear as he wondered what she had gone through as a kid.

Her obvious uneasiness made his gut churn. He actually felt the need to grip the tea mug in both his hands to keep from touching her, soothing her, even though he didn't know yet what she was about to reveal.

"I went into foster care at such an early age," she continued, "I have no memories whatsoever of either of my parents."

Abby was an orphan. Just like his little Sona. The revelation created a frown on his brow that bit deeply into his forehead.

Almost as if reading his thoughts, Abby clarified, "I wasn't actually an orphan." She looked away as if it were painful for her to admit. "I was abandoned."

Heaving a deep sigh, she continued, "I was shuffled from foster home to foster home. That's all I remember. Making new friends and having those friends ripped out of my life after a few months or a year."

Her gaze shifted from the far corner of the room to the tea in her mug. "I did have some good experiences. Most of the adults who cared for me were kindhearted, generous people willing to open their homes to homeless kids. But some of the foster homes were run by people just looking to make a buck off the state. Taking in foster kids was a way to do it. And they'd make a profit by feeding us the most inexpensive food they could find. Supplying us with the most low-cost clothing and shoes.''

Ethan watched as her eyes glazed over with the unpleasant past. He doubted that she was even aware that he was sitting next to her, so absorbed did she become in her story.

''I have to say, I was very lucky,'' she continued. ''I was only in one abusive home. The foster parents were very strict. Disciplinarians, they called themselves. I guess I deserved the punishment I got.''

Her voice grew faint and far-off, and Ethan knew she'd become totally lost in the past.

''I remember one spanking well,'' she whispered. ''I hadn't made my bed. I knew it was an important rule. The law, really. You didn't come down to breakfast unless your bed was made. But I'd overslept and I would have gotten into trouble if I'd been late for school.''

Her beautiful face scrunched up with the indecision she must have felt as a child. Which rule should she break? Not making the bed? Or being late for school?

Ethan's heart split as he contemplated the rock-and-a-hard-place Abby was describing herself stuck in as a child.

''My third-grade teacher noticed the welt that the belt had left on my leg and she called Social Services.'' Her chin tipped up a fraction. ''I was taken out of that foster home immediately.''

''Good.'' Ethan couldn't contain the blurted response. ''I hope the state closed down the home.''

She blinked twice, as though his voice jerked her back to the present.

"Oh, I'm sure they didn't," she was quick to answer. "The need for foster parents was too great. Too many kids. Too few homes. I'm sure the people were warned, but—" she shrugged "—that probably changed nothing."

"But that's ridiculous!" He felt angry. Outraged. At the people who had hurt Abby. At the state for allowing the treatment to continue on other innocent children.

But these things had happened to Abby so long ago. His anger drained away until nothing was left but a nagging sadness.

"Something wonderful happened when I was in the seventh grade." Her face brighten considerably with a smile. "I had a teacher who played some Spanish tapes for the class. The next day, I came to school speaking some Spanish. Even putting some words together to make sentences. For some reason, the words and phrases just stuck in my head. Mr. Callahan was amazed. He ended up working with me all year. We listened to French records and cassettes. And then Italian. Russian. All kinds of languages. It seemed very easy for me to pick them up. It was like a game to me."

The wonder expressed on her face made her more gorgeous than ever. Ethan sucked in his breath, waiting for her to continue.

"I moved out of the school district," she said, "so I lost track of Mr. Callahan. But I never lost my love of languages. I took French and Italian in high school. The counselor didn't want me to. She tried to tell me the classes would be too much. That one foreign language would be enough for me to handle. But I proved to her I could do it. And I continued to learn other languages on my own.'' She grinned. ''I earned a full scholarship through state college. But I already told you that.''

Setting her tea mug down on the coffee table, she said, ''Whoever gave me this wonderful gift—God, or Fate, or Mother Nature...'' She shook her head. ''It saved me. Gave me something on which to focus my energy. It gave me direction. And a way out.''

There was something hauntingly sad in her last statement, he thought, something that needed pondering. But he didn't take the time to think it through. The urge to talk to Abby was too great. He quietly said, ''And now you use your gift to teach other kids.''

She nodded, and went silent. But her mind was still churning with the past. Sensing that she had more to say, he waited.

''I did go looking for my parents,'' she told him.

He could see the sorrow and rejection she'd so very obviously experienced even before she spoke.

''When I was eighteen, I went to Child Services.'' Her jaw tensed. ''What I discovered is that there's no known information about my father at all. Not a name or an address. Nothing. My mother listed my father's name on my birth certificate as John Doe. She gave me up to the state the day I was born. She'd signed a paper refusing to have information about herself released. To me. To anyone. Ever. The state's hands were tied. They couldn't tell me a thing.''

She suppressed her anguish well. But Ethan

couldn't help but perceive it, be deeply affected by it. This woman needed to be held. Needed to be hugged. Needed some physical consolation.

Setting down his mug, he slid over and gathered her up in his arms. And there was not one nuance of hesitation in her as she allowed herself to be enfolded in his embrace.

"It's okay," he whispered against her sweet-smelling hair. "There's not a whole lot you can do about the choices two people made years and years ago. Who knows what kind of circumstances they were in? It could be that they were very young and unable to…"

He let the sentence trail, realizing that nothing he could say would lessen Abby's pain. There were no words that could take away her feeling of rejection. No matter what situation he might explain, no matter what sympathetic picture he might try to paint to explain her parent's behavior. So he simply hugged Abby to him, not really understanding what he hoped to accomplish. Maybe this close contact would somehow make up, just a little, for all the love and compassion she'd missed throughout her childhood.

Long minutes passed, and Abby seemed content to take refuge in his arms. She didn't cry, but he could feel the sorrow fairly oozing from her. He rubbed his palms up and down her back in a slow, rhythmic motion.

Soon, Ethan became aware of the softness of her skin beneath his fingertips, the warm, meadow-flower fragrance of her body so close to his, the feel of her firm breasts pressed against his chest.

This wasn't the time for him to feel aroused. But, heaven help him, that's exactly what he felt.

And this was no gentle, slow-growing germination of passion. Fiery desire reared its head seemingly out of nowhere. Rolling over him in a flash. Nearly crushing him, like a huge wall of water. One instant he was full of concern, the next he was brimming with a need so fierce it almost stole away his breath.

His blood pulsed thicker and hotter with each passing second. He wanted to tip back his head, to savor the sight of her pale-as-porcelain face, gaze into her gem-green eyes, kiss her rose-wine lips, until there was no trace of sadness left in her.

But he couldn't do that. This wasn't the time. Or the place.

Then he remembered that there wouldn't *ever* be a right time or place. Not with Abby. She was too good, too fragile, for the likes of him. The few women he had chosen to date knew up front that he didn't intend to commit himself. He favored women who could take care of themselves. Who were just as...selfish and self-serving as he. That way, when he was ready to end a relationship, which he invariably did, he felt comfortable that the woman would be okay. That he wouldn't leave her feeling hurt and floundering.

Abby wasn't in that class. She was vulnerable. Loving. Caring. He'd end up hurting her for sure. So he had to rein in these physical feelings. He simply *had* to.

He felt the flat of her palm against his chest as she gently pushed herself away from him. Lifting her chin, she looked into his eyes. Ethan thought he was going to melt under the heat of her gaze. She studied his lips, then returned her gaze to his.

She was feeling as passionate as he. That fact shined as clear and bright as a beautiful spring morning.

The urge to kiss her walloped him like a sucker punch right to his gut. He all but doubled over from its force. But he refused to surrender. This woman meant too much to him. Meant too much to his little girl.

The soul-wrenching hunger reflected in Abby's exquisite expression matched his own. They both wanted this moment to develop into...something more. Yet neither followed through on the need that was so obviously pulsing through them. Neither was willing to cross that line. To take that first step.

Abby's motives for hesitating weren't completely clear to him. He had lots of pieces to the puzzle of who she was, how she thought, but he hadn't quite put them all together.

Ethan, on the other hand, knew without a doubt why he didn't act. His reasons were sound. Strong. And right.

Finally, she swallowed, and pushed herself farther away from him. His arms slid from around her, his hands dropping to his sides.

"You're a good man," she whispered. "A very good man."

Gratitude tinged her tone, and it actually made him feel a bit chagrined about the deep desire throbbing in him, about the passion that continued to push him toward the edge of sanity. He didn't feel like a good man. The hunger pulsing through him had him feeling anything but.

"Thanks for letting me..."

Her shy hesitation was sweet.

"...lean on you."

Ethan's exhalation was slow and even as he worked to control all that he was feeling. There was just something about this woman that brought out the protector in him. The big, tough guy who was willing to take on the world.

"Anytime, Abby," he told her softly. "You know that."

But she looked away as if she didn't...or as if she didn't want to. He wanted to groan. He hated to think that the awkwardness might creep up between them again.

As if sensing his thoughts, she said, "Enough of this miserable talk of the past. Tell me what you found out today. About the annulment."

Ethan stifled a sigh, grateful to have a subject of conversation that was manageable, businesslike. This, he could handle.

"Well," he responded, "I found out that it'll be pretty easy. And pretty swift. My lawyer will start filing the papers tomorrow. And as long as both of us can state that there was no...um...ah...you know—" He suddenly stumbled over the words. "As long as there's no...physical relationship, no consummation, we'll be just fine."

She tried to hide her embarrassment, but he couldn't help but think how cute she looked with her cheeks tinted pink.

"We knew that, though, didn't we?" she asked,

avoiding his eyes. "There hasn't been any trouble there."

He wondered how she could say that with what they had both experienced just thirty seconds before. He'd certainly had trouble keeping his hands to himself. Oh, well, he decided, attesting to false facts might make the truth easier to ignore.

They spent a few more moments talking about the legal ins and outs of the annulment, and when the subject waned, Abby said, "I really should say goodnight. It's getting late. You'd better get to bed, too. The sun will be rising before you know it."

"I know," he told her. "I'll head upstairs in just a few minutes."

She took their mugs with her, offering to put them in the sink on her way through the kitchen.

The TV continued to drone softly in the quiet once Ethan was all alone.

He felt exhausted. As if he'd fought some huge battle…and had won. He knew the struggle had been against himself. Against his own physical wants and desires. Against his growing passion for Abby.

He was confident that he could fight the physical attraction he felt for her again, should the need arise. And he was fairly certain the need *would* arise. Heck, if willpower alone wasn't enough, there was always a long, icy shower just waiting to be utilized.

However, he was a little more concerned with the *other* attraction for her that had begun to stir in him. She conjured emotions in him he really didn't want to feel…*couldn't afford* to feel and continue to remain detached and objective about their relationship.

Yes, a good, cold shower might take care of the

physical attraction that plagued him. But what about the emotion attraction? What about the feelings in his gut, in his heart, that continued to linger long after the needs of his body had once again grown manageable?

An afternoon bubble bath. The very idea was decadent.

Abby stretched out in the tub, water lapping at her toes, belly and breasts, frothy bubbles tickling every inch of exposed skin. She closed her eyes, indulging completely in the luxury of simply being lazy. She sighed contentedly, sinking deeper into the water, doubting that anyone but the most wealthy citizens of Kyrcznovia even owned a bath tub, let alone took long, lazy soaks. She knew *she* hadn't enjoyed such an extravagance since...she had to stop and think...wow, she couldn't even remember when.

Sona was napping, Ethan was busy on his computer. And Abby was relaxing with a good book in a bubbly, wet paradise. She didn't think life could get more blissful than this.

Inevitably, Ethan entered her thoughts. And suddenly, her brain was filled with memories of how he had held her last night. Closing her fingers around the airy bubbles, she remembered the feel of his hard chest under her palms, the deliciously warm scent of him as he'd hugged her close. She easily pictured the desire that had danced in his mahogany eyes. Lowering her lids, she felt her body respond to the need he conjured in her. Her skin tingled all over, her belly heated deep down inside.

Slowly, she ran her fingertips over her flat tummy

and then up toward her breasts, imagining it was Ethan's touch she was feeling. Her nipples budded. Her breath quickened. Oh, how she wanted him. And *he* wanted her. She had known it. Had seen it in his eyes, felt it in the tenseness of his body.

Her eyes flew open and she swallowed nervously as that odd dismay filled her like a hazy fog, making her feel heavy and afraid. Why did she always experience this awful—

The thump she heard had her eyes widening. What was that? A door slamming? A...

The sound of heavy footfalls on the steps had her sitting up in the tub with such force that water sloshed onto the floor.

"Ethan?" she called. "What is it?"'

Then Abby heard Sona's ear-piercing cry.

Having lived in this house for more than two weeks, Abby knew Sona had many different cries. The little girl would give a whiny cry if she wanted attention, an angry cry if she was frustrated. She'd whimper when she was tired, or tearfully complain if she was hungry. But this was clearly an expression of pain.

Hopping out of the tub, Abby was heedless of the water and soapy bubbles dripping onto the floor as she snatched up a towel. She wrapped it around herself haphazardly and jerked open the door.

She barreled into Sona's room and saw Ethan standing at the crib, his daughter in his arms.

"Oh, Ethan!" Her voice was shaky with fear. "What happened?"

"She tried to climb out of her crib. She fell to the floor. Thank God she's not seriously hurt."

The guilt in his gaze was so thick, Abby wanted to reach out to soothe him. And that's exactly what she did. Placing one hand on his arm, the other against Sona's back, Abby said, "There's no way we could have known this was going to happen."

"She could have broken her neck," he said. "I've got to lower the crib mattress. There's got to be a way to do it...."

"I'm sure there is," she told him, the heavy self-blame in his tone ripping like claws at her soul. "But right now, we ought to get some ice on that boo-boo on her noggin."

Abby hoped the playful term she'd used for Sona's injury would lighten the mood, but Ethan refused to be consoled. In fact, she quickly discovered she'd only made him feel worse.

"Of course!" he said, rushing toward the door. "How could I be so stupid? I should put a cold compress on her forehead."

They rushed down the stairs and through the house to the kitchen. Abby felt terrible that in mentioning the ice she'd only made him feel even more down on himself.

"The floor is carpeted," she reminded him above Sona's cries. "She couldn't have fallen too hard."

With his free hand, Ethan pulled open the freezer door.

"Here," Abby said, "let me get that."

She placed several ice cubes in a plastic bag and then surrounded it with a soft, clean dish towel. It took them several moments to get Sona to allow them to apply the ice to the angry red bump on her head.

Ethan pulled out a chair and sat with Sona on his knee. Abby kneeled down beside them, trying to divert the child's attention from what her daddy was doing. Sona had stopped sobbing, but she continued to whine and fidget.

"Well, at least she doesn't seem to be in a lot of pain," Abby pointed out to Ethan.

"Yeah, but there's still fear in her eyes. I bet that fall scared the wits out of her."

Abby could only nod. "Daddy will fix your crib, sweetie," she crooned to Sona who had squirmed around to face her.

"I should have set the mattress to the lowest position when I put together the damned crib," he said. "If I had, this wouldn't have happened."

"Yes, but you'd have strained your back trying to get Sona in and out of bed," Abby gently pointed out.

"Better that then having her fall and break her arm or something."

He felt terribly responsible for his daughter's accident, and Abby felt awful about that.

"Ethan—" she placed her hand on his knee "—you're not going to be able to keep Sona safe every moment of every day. You'll keep her as safe as you can, but it's inevitable…stuff is going to happen."

Ethan just studied her, worry darkening his eyes.

"I remember," she continued, "in one of the foster homes where I grew up, there had been a safety gate placed at the head of a flight of stairs. A little boy—he was about Sona's age, maybe a little older—managed to climb over the gate. He fell down the stairs." She looked off, remembering the awful scene. "He broke his nose. And he got an awful black eye."

She sighed, shoved the memory aside and looked up at Ethan whose gaze had shifted and was directed at the floor.

"The house was full of people," she told him, "yet nobody saw that child climbing over the gate. Kids just have a way of getting into things they shouldn't. They just have a way of finding trouble."

Still he remained silent. So did Sona.

Ethan's utter stillness, his inability to respond, told Abby just how upset he was with himself, how culpable he felt that his daughter had been hurt.

She rubbed small circles on his knee, patted it twice, then rubbed again as she softly said, "You can't beat yourself up about this. We'll fix the crib so she can't climb out. Everything's going to be okay." He still refused to look at her. "It really is," she assured him. "Honest."

At that moment, Sona reached out and scooped a small mound of bubbles that had been clinging to Abby's bare shoulder. The little girl giggled when the delicate bubbles popped and disappeared from her fingertips.

Abby's eyes went wide, remembering suddenly that she'd been bathing when she heard the commotion in Sona's room. She looked down the length of her towel-clad body. The soft terry fabric parted high on her thigh, exposing a wedge of her white flesh. When she looked up into Ethan's face, she realized in that instant that he wasn't focused on the floor as he silently condemned himself—*he'd been giving her bare legs an intense and ogling stare.*

Abby was mortified. She gasped and jerked herself upright, tugging and pulling in some vain attempt to get the towel to cover more of herself than was reasonably possible.

Ethan was obviously just as mortified as she, his eyes going as wide as saucers as his gaze latched onto her face. However, his chagrin quickly melted away, and she could see him fighting hard to suppress the sudden, and evidently unexpected, merriment that began to dance in his luscious nut-brown eyes.

She should feel humiliated by his leering. She should feel angry. She should feel appalled. Shocked. Infuriated. She should be feeling anything except...except...*flattered.*

Abby would not smile at the way his mouth was curling at the corners, teasing and sexy. She would not!

But no sooner had the thought entered her head when her own lips were being tugged at by the makings of a beguiling grin. But she shouldn't. *She just shouldn't.*

Suddenly overcome with the irrepressible seduction scene that had materialized seemingly out of very air itself, Abby opened her mouth to take in a quick breath.

Ethan was flirting with her, she could see it in his hungry eyes, in the sensual set of his mouth. He *wanted* her. A thrill shot through her, and then that vague, bone-chilling fear followed closely on its heels.

"I—I was in the tub." The obvious truth came out sounding like a lame excuse. She knew it, heard it, as soon as the words left her mouth. "Wh-when I heard Sona fall, I—I was scared witless. I d-didn't know what had happened." Why couldn't she speak five full words without stuttering? Never before had she suffered with a speech impediment. Clearing her throat, she stammered, "I—I didn't stop to…" Sheer frustration made the thought fade into oblivion.

His brazen smile only widened. "I can see that."

The rich, lazy sound of his timbre caused a shiver to course across every inch of her skin. She broke out in gooseflesh and she felt her nipples contract into nubs. His eyes traveling her body were almost as tangible as his touch, and after the very erotic thoughts she'd had of him only moments before in the tub…

Her throat convulsed and she automatically crossed her arms over her chest. There was really no gracious way to do this and not allow him to become privy to the exact reaction she was trying to hide.

"I—I really should go upstairs," she stammered. "I should—"

"Yes." He nodded, his now full, lopsided grin helplessly expanding with each millisecond that passed. "You *really* should."

She turned and darted from the kitchen, his delighted laughter ringing in her ears.

Chapter Eight

Ethan was thoroughly enjoying the change in his relationship with Abby. And he knew the bubbles-and-terry-cloth incident—which was how he'd dubbed the situation when Abby had come running out of her bath a couple of days ago clad only in a few well-placed bubbles and a too short terry towel—had been the turning point.

They were playful with one another. Friendly and flirtatious. It was refreshing and fun, and Ethan refused to even consider, let alone contemplate, all the implications of the change. He only focused—for the time being—on relishing it.

He checked the saddle on Blaze, and then did the same on Pepper. Abby was dressing Sona, and then the three of them planned to ride into the park and share a picnic breakfast. These kinds of spur-of-the-moment happenings were the very reason he felt so blessed that he owned his own business and worked out of his home. When most men and women were fighting traffic on the Blue Route, he was sipping his coffee, enjoying the morning, or exercising one or the other of his horses in the parkland surrounding his home. Yes, he was truly blessed.

Ethan realized that Abby, too, was a blessing in his life. If she hadn't happened into that hotel restaurant in Kyrcznovia looking for a job, he was sure he wouldn't have custody of Sona right now. He owed Abby a lot. And after hearing about her background, about her childhood, Ethan only felt more protective of her—more attracted to her—than ever. The urge to offer her a little happiness while she was in America seemed to drown out all the doubts and qualms and hesitations he'd felt up to this point.

Sure, the fact that neither of them were looking for long-term involvement, or even romantic entanglements, was still in his mind. But that didn't mean that he and Abby couldn't have some good times together with Sona. That they couldn't make some pleasant memories together. Some happy reflections she could cherish after she was gone. Just as he would.

After she was gone...

The words echoed in his head. His arms relaxed at his sides and his gaze lowered to study the straw at his feet. The concept of his house vacant of Abby made him feel—

"We're ready!"

Abby's bright-and-cheery voice jarred him out of his somber contemplation. Sona squealed a delighted greeting to Ethan and then automatically reached out, straining to touch Blaze's nose.

"You do love these horses, don't you, pumpkin?"
Ethan smoothed Sona's dark hair back from her face.

"Are you sure the harness is going to work?"
Abby asked him.

He nodded, knowing she was speaking of the
backpack-type child seat he'd bought so he could
take Sona out on the horse. "Everything will be
fine," he told Abby. "We'll take it nice and slow.
Get her used to riding Blaze. And get me used to
carrying her on horseback."

He found Abby's concern charming. Heck, he was
finding there was little about her that he didn't find
captivating.

When she didn't respond right away, he grinned
at her and teased, "Are you doubting me?"

"Oh, no," she said. Then she chuckled. "If anyone can handle riding a horse while carrying a baby
on his back, it's you." Then Abby looked at his
daughter, "Isn't that right, Sona? We have plenty of
faith in your daddy. There's not much he can't handle."

Her praise made his chest swell. However, he
couldn't help but wonder if her too bright tone meant
that a shadow of worry might be clouding the confidence she espoused.

Crooking his index finger under Abby's chin, he
tipped up her face until she was forced to look him
in the eye. "Everything will be fine," he promised
softly.

The cool morning air crackled and snapped with
electricity. Finally, she smiled demurely and said,
"I'm sure it will be."

That soft-and-sunny smile did strange things to his

libido. Ethan thought his heart was going to thump right out of his chest cavity. Lord, but she was lovely.

He shrugged the straps of the harness over his shoulders and then Abby secured Sona into the canvas contraption. All the while, the child clapped and giggled, knowing something exciting was about to take place.

Blaze and Pepper were led out into the sunshine of the paddock, and Abby asked Ethan, "Everything's packed?"

"Yes."

With Sona strapped to his back, he wasn't much help to Abby as she mounted Pepper, but he placed a steadying hand on her thigh once she got her leg over the saddle. Liquid fire shot straight up his arm.

"Bagels and juice and fruit. All packed in your saddlebags." He was utterly amazed that he was able to respond in such a normal manner.

"I'm a beginner at this riding stuff, myself," Abby reminded him, patting his hand where it rested on her leg.

With the heat of her firm thigh beneath his hand, the softness of her warm palm above it, he was sure his entire body would burst into flame at any moment. Spontaneous combustion. He slid his hand free and took a backward step.

He grinned as he gathered Blaze's reins in his hand, hoping to cover the chaotic physical response to her nearness. "I'll remember that I have two amateurs with me this morning."

They experienced one hair-raising moment when Sona cried out in fear as Ethan hoisted himself up into the saddle. But once they were settled and he'd murmured some assurances to his daughter, she quieted, her tiny hands gripping her daddy's shoulders.

The trails were dappled with sunlight and colorful flowers sprouted here and there among the lush, green underbrush. Oak trees towered above them, offering them cool shade from the summer heat.

After a twenty-minute ride during which they had met only a solitary jogger on the wide-open paths of the park, Ethan suggested, "How 'bout we stop here and eat?"

"Sounds good," Abby told him. Making the dismount look as sweet as a slice of apple pie, she hopped to the ground and looped Pepper's reins over a low-hanging branch.

Meaning to warn Sona that they were about to dismount, Ethan said, "We're getting down, sweetheart." Without waiting for Abby to translate his words, he swung his leg over the saddle.

Pain shot through his head and he squished his eyes shut, grimacing.

"Whoa," he cried out, reaching up and gently encircling his daughter's little wrists.

Abby clapped a quelling hand over her mouth, but not in time to hold back her impulsive laughter. Ignoring the subsiding pain, he cocked his head and fixed her with a glare that had her trying even more valiantly to suppress her humor.

"Well," she finally said, "I think Sona found the perfect safety handles."

"Those are not handles," he said, gritting his teeth as he extricated himself from his daughter's death grip. "They're my *ears*."

Amusement evidently got the best of Abby and she broke out in gales of laughter. Sona joined in, seemingly quite delighted that she'd caused such a stir in the adults.

"Would you please help get this little urchin off my back?" he asked.

Abby continued to chortle intermittently as she unfastened Sona's restraining belt and pulled the child free. All Ethan could do was rub his flaming ears.

Sona toddled off toward the picnic table, stopping along the way to investigate pinecones and pebbles and whatever else she could find on the ground. Ethan tried to wiggle out of the harness, but one strap caught on his shoulder. Without being asked, Abby came to his rescue. She pulled the canvas harness off his back and tossed it over his horse's saddle.

Planting his hands on his waist, he arched his back, stretching the muscles. He bent his neck one way then the other, working out the strain and kinks. Sensing Abby slipping up behind him, he stilled when he felt the warmth of her palms slide over his tense shoulder muscles.

She kneaded his neck and upper back, digging her thumbs in at just the right places. He was able to stifle the groan of gratification that welled in his throat, but he did allow his eyelids to ease shut. Abby had magic fingers. However, her gentle touch alone—without any rubbing or massaging—would have made him dizzy with pleasure. *Sensual* pleasure.

Then he felt her featherlight fingertips gently tracing the outer rim of his left ear. His throat went dry and he stopped breathing, waiting.

"The redness is going away," she whispered. Her tone turned light and deliciously teasing as she added. "I do believe you're going to live."

Her voice was close behind him, and it sent a luscious chill raking down every single vertebra of his spine. Wisps of fire flickered deep in his belly, licking at him, rousing a heated passion within him. He wanted to hold her close. Inhale the scent of her hair and skin. Touch the full length of her elegant neck with his fingers, with his lips. And in that one insane instant, he surrendered to the urges that tormented him.

With no warning, he turned, smiling at the surprise that registered on her lovely face, grasping her upper arms so she couldn't step away from him. Her emerald eyes went wide, and the desire flaring inside him forced his smile to wane.

"The morning sunlight turns your hair to copper flames," he murmured, sure that the metaphor was provoked by the profound fire burning in him—the fire that blazed hotter with each passing second.

Ethan pulled her up against his chest, barely touched his nose to her temple. "And you smell wonderful."

She felt small in his arms. Delicate. And quivery. Like a fragile flower bud. Coaxing that bud to open to him suddenly seemed the most important goal on this earth.

He ran the tip of his nose down along her face, from temple to jaw line and then back up, daring to stroke her cheekbone with first the feathery touch of his chin, and then the light press of his lips. Her skin was as smooth as alabaster.

Inhaling deeply, fully, he was content at this moment to simply be near her. However, that contentment diminished swiftly, and he felt a terrible need to taste her, to touch her.

Sliding his fingers up behind her ear and into her silky tresses, he studied her eyes, wanting to gauge her reaction to what was happening between them. Wanting to gauge her reaction *to him.*

His newly formed daddy instinct had him darting a quick glance at his daughter, who was busying herself gathering a pile of pinecones and acorns, so Ethan felt safe focusing his attention once more on Abby, assessing her response, discovering exactly what it was she was feeling.

Her expression was unreadable at first. Filled with a dark and thrilling mystery he wanted desperately to solve. Then he deciphered multilayers of complex emotion.

Uncertainty. Confusion. Wonder. Astonishment. Doubt. Was that a touch of fear? he wondered.

Then he saw it. Desire. Rich, heady and deep.

The passion he read in her gaze wavered, seemed to teeter on the very edge of her consciousness, as if she wasn't sure she should—*or even wanted to*—feel it. But it was there in her eyes, in her shallow breath, in her trembling body.

As if to confirm his thoughts, she softly whispered, "We shouldn't, Ethan. We really shouldn't."

When she spoke the word *shouldn't,* her luscious lips puckered oh-so-slightly and he felt that if he didn't kiss her—then and there—that he'd surely shrivel into nothingness and disappear completely.

"I don't give a damn," he said, the overwhelming

passion turning his tone to a growl. Staring deeply into her eyes, he asked, "Do you?"

The need pulsing through her evidently matched his own for, without hesitation, she shook her head back and forth once, twice, and then she relaxed into his arms.

She tasted faintly sweet, like warm mint, and Ethan savored the pleasant flavor of her. Her mouth was soft and pliant and hot, the taste and feel and scent of her making his body grow feverish.

Breaking away from him, she whispered against his mouth, "Sona."

Her concern for his little girl—right in the midst of their all-consuming passion—made him want to only hug her harder, kiss her more. Abby was a marvelous human being.

"She's fine," he assured her, casting another quick look at Sona to be sure he was telling the truth. His sweet angel baby was separating the pinecones and acorns into piles. He looked at Abby, who had closed her eyes, seemingly enjoying this forbidden caress just as much as he.

Maybe he should allow sanity a foothold in his brain. Maybe he should release Abby and embark on the impossible task of forgetting that this kiss ever happened. However, the need to hold her, to kiss her, had plagued him for *so very long*. For the first time in weeks, he felt his agony subside...all because holding her in his arms was having his craving satiated. So he just couldn't bring himself to give up this precious moment by setting her free just yet.

He kissed one delicate eyelid. And then the other. One corner of her mouth. And then the other.

She opened her eyes, and for a single instant, Ethan felt as if their souls connected. It was then that he knew.

He was falling in love.

Dr. Smyth listened to Sona's heart and then pressed the stethoscope to her back. The pediatrician smiled at Ethan when Sona squirmed and giggled.

"She sure is a happy child," the doctor commented.

Ethan only nodded nervously. He wasn't going to allow the good doctor to distract him. He'd heard about infant immunizations, and he wasn't looking forward to the ones that were surely in his daughter's imminent future.

"A lot of toddlers usually scream bloody murder during their first visit to my office." The doctor set Sona on the scale and leaned over to fiddle with the weights until an accurate reading registered.

Ethan's palms felt clammy and he unwittingly rubbed them down the length of his khaki-covered thighs. He didn't like the idea that Dr. Smyth was going to hurt his little girl with needles, even though he realized that the tiny bit of pain was necessary and just might save Sona's life in the years to come. Still, he couldn't help feeling reluctant.

"Hmmm," the doctor murmured. "Her weight is on the low end of the spectrum."

Ethan's ears pricked up. "Is that bad?"

"Well, Sona looks healthy."

"She's very healthy," he rushed to say. "As far as I know."

Dr. Smyth nodded, not taking her attention off

Ethan's daughter. The woman held up a ball and seemed pleased when Sona reached for it.

"Her sight and coordination seem normal," the doctor observed. "My guess is she didn't get a whole lot to eat during her time in the orphanage." She glanced at Ethan. "How has she been eating since you brought her home?"

"She eats like a horse."

The doctor smiled. "Good. I'll just make a note on her chart that will remind us to keep a close eye on her weight."

The examination continued for several moments, and Ethan's mind was once again nagged by the idea of those needles that he knew loomed in the very close future…like in the next five to ten minutes.

Placing Sona on the floor, the doctor encouraged the child to walk around the tiny room. "Her balance is great. She walks well. Like any other toddler her age."

Finally, Ethan could hold in his anxiety no longer. "Let's talk about Sona's inoculations."

Dr. Smyth seemed taken aback by his abruptness and he felt heat suffuse his face.

"Okay," the pediatrician answered. "We can talk about her baby shots now, if you like."

Even though he tried to relax, he felt his muscles tense, his jaw tighten.

The doctor studied Sona's chart. Then she said, "As you know, your daughter received some of the necessary inoculations and her tuberculosis skin test before she was allowed to enter the country. However, there are a few she still needs to get started on."

"Started on?" He didn't like the sound of that.

Dr. Smyth nodded. "Immunizations are given in doses. Some of them take three. Some take four. And they're given over a span of twelve to eighteen months."

A frown bit into his brow at the prospect of having to suffer through this anxiety on pretty much an ongoing basis for the next year and a half.

Evidently the good doctor noticed his nervous apprehension. "I promise, Mr. Kimball—" she hesitated long enough to grin at him "—I won't prick you even once with a needle."

He smiled at her attempt to allay his apprehension, but the thought of seeing Sona cry still shadowed his thoughts.

"You know," Dr. Smyth continued, "maybe your wife should be in here with you and your daughter...."

"Oh, no—" his head shook back and forth quickly "—Abby...the lady in the waiting room...isn't my wife. She's, um, our nanny."

The *our* sounded kind of silly, he thought as soon as the plural possessive had tumbled off his tongue. But that's how he'd thought of Abby from the first day he'd met her. In a way that was quite personal. Special. So he really didn't care how it sounded.

"Ah, I see...well," the doctor said, obviously intent on making a second try. "Maybe you'd like for her to be back here, anyway. You know, as a kind of moral support for both you and your daughter."

The suggestion caused his whole body to react. He grew calmer immediately, and after moistening his lips, he sighed.

"You know," he said, "I think that would be a great idea."

Even though the doctor wielded the syringe with swift expertise, Sona still cried. Abby and Ethan both did what they could to comfort her as the doctor took a moment to jot down her final notes in the file.

"You did a great job, Sona," Dr. Smyth said, smoothing a loving hand down the child's arm.

But Sona only hid her face in the crook of her daddy's neck.

"Mr. Kimball, my secretary will set you up for your next appointment in two months."

Once the doctor left the three of them alone, Abby immediately reached for Sona's clothing.

"Oh, Lord," Ethan helplessly murmured. "I hate the idea of coming back here. No wonder children scream bloody murder."

"Scream bloody murder?" Abby asked as she slipped a sock onto Sona's little foot.

"It was something the doctor said before you came in," he told her. "That her patients scream bloody murder. What I find amazing is that the parents of her patients don't scream. And kick. And run for their lives."

Abby chuckled. "When Dr. Smyth came toward Sona with that needle, I thought sure you were going to do just that. Run for your life." She quickly sobered. "It's necessary, you know."

He nodded, resignedly. "I do know." He cradled the back of his daughter's head with the palm of his hand. "It's just that...I thought my job was pretty clearly mapped out. To protect this precious child from harm."

"And you're doing that," Abby told him gently. "By bringing her here."

Again, he nodded. "But I felt so awful. So guilty."

Abby roused Sona from Ethan's protective embrace long enough to tug the child's dress over her little head. Then Abby fastened the button at the back.

"I have to admit," Abby said. "I thought my heart was going to break when I saw Sona begin to cry. But Dr. Smyth did her best to be quick."

He looked at Abby and felt a rush of relief that she was here to share this miserable experience with him.

The three of them went out into the reception area and Abby took Sona from Ethan so he could write out a check to pay for the office visit. As he waited for a receipt, he became acutely aware of Abby standing by his elbow as she gently rocked Sona back and forth.

Since discovering his deep feelings for Abby, he'd felt torn. On one hand, he wanted to tell her. He wanted to see if she might be willing to make a go at a real relationship with him. But on the other hand…he knew he should keep his mouth shut about his feelings.

Was he willing to see her hurt? Because if he was to become involved with Abby, that was the sure outcome. Pain and distress for her.

Who was he kidding? he silently asked himself. "The other hand" was the only hand—the only *choice*—he had. He simply must keep his mouth shut.

The receptionist handed Ethan the receipt and the piece of paper that noted the date of Sona's next visit. He murmured a farewell, and then turned to Abby. His breath caught as he looked into her clear, beautiful eyes.

And he wondered how on earth he was going to be able to keep silent about what was in his heart.

Chapter Nine

"Hi, Bob," Abby called out as she entered the barn.

The reserved caretaker nodded a silent greeting and then continued his task of spreading fresh hay in Blaze's stall.

The elderly man did his job, and did it well, without an abundance of conversation. Heck, without practically any conversation. Bob Davis was definitely a man of few words. And that's why Abby felt safe coming into the barn to do the thinking she needed to do.

"Would you mind if I help you with the grooming today?" she asked the caretaker.

"That'd be fine," he said, casting her only a cursory glance.

Pepper's stall smelled of sweet, fresh hay and warm horseflesh. Abby greeted the animal with a soft hello as she smoothed her palm down the length of the animal's neck. The grooming brush felt a bit heavy in her hand, but Abby quickly got used to the weight of it as she ran the bristles over the horse.

The two weeks that had passed since she and Ethan had shared that soul-shattering kiss in the park had been the most wonderful of her life. She knew in her heart that the flirtatiousness between them didn't—no, *couldn't*—mean anything. Ethan had told her early on, when she'd suggested he find himself a mate, that he simply wasn't interested in a relationship. And even if he was, Abby knew she wouldn't be staying here much longer. In fact, she'd received word that there was a teaching position for her in Slovakia. Seems she was needed immediately, but the job would be held for her for two weeks. She'd come out to the barn to plan the best way to tell Ethan.

Another week here with him and Sona should be sufficient, she surmised. Then she could fly to Slovakia with time to spare, time to find a place to live, before starting the job.

With each day that passed, Ethan seemed more and more comfortable in his new role as Sona's daddy. And the toddler seemed so happy in her new home here in America. Before too much longer, neither one of them would need Abby. However, that had been the whole idea from the beginning.

So, this flirtation she and Ethan had been enjoying would soon be coming to an end. It might only have been temporary, but it sure had been fun! She hadn't ever—in her whole life—felt such delight, such pure, playful joy as she'd felt when she'd participated in their impish banter or when she'd been in Ethan's arms or felt his mouth pressed against her own.

Pepper nickered softly, seeming to sense the light-heartedness that had Abby's mouth curling into a whispery smile.

However, a small, dark cloud seemed to form over her when she thought about telling Ethan about the job that was waiting for her. Surely, he'd be happy for her. Surely, he'd accept the news with—

Bob gave a soft cough and said, "I, ah..."

Pleasantly surprised by the caretaker's obvious intention to talk with her, Abby looked his way, her hand resting on Pepper's silky back.

"I've been meaning to tell you," he continued. "I don't ever think I've seen Ethan so happy. He's usually stuck in that office of his twelve or fourteen hours a day. And now he's going shopping and taking picnics out in the park. It's really great."

Abby blinked, once, twice. This was the most she'd ever heard Bob speak since meeting him weeks ago.

"He *is* happy," Abby agreed. "Sona has really changed his life."

The elderly caretaker cleared his throat. "If you don't mind my saying so, I tend to think little Sona isn't the only reason behind his good spirits."

Embarrassment warmed her cheeks. He was evidently hinting that she was behind the change in Ethan. She felt the need to stop this before it even started. The man needed to be told the truth. She couldn't stay here.

Why not? The tiny question echoed in her head.

But she shoved it aside just the way she did every other time it had plagued her.

Slipping her palm from under the leather strap, she set the grooming brush aside and moved to the chin-high wall at the front end of the stall.

"You know, Bob," she said, "I'm not going to be staying here. I have a job to go to in Slovakia. I'll be leaving soon. I only came here to make Sona's transition go a little smoother."

Bob stopped spreading the hay and planted the rake on the barn floor. He gazed up at her for the first time. "Ethan did tell me that. But it's just that…" His words seemed to falter. "Well, it just seemed to me that…things had changed."

The saucy fun she and Ethan had been having with one another might have been entirely innocent in their minds, but it was obvious that their behavior toward one another had been noticed by Bob, and it had altered the caretaker's perception of the situation.

When she didn't respond, he said, "Now I don't mean to be forward, and I probably shouldn't be sticking my nose into your business, but—" his shoulder lifted slightly in a small shrug "—having a woman in his life has been good for Ethan. I'm afraid he might not tell you that. So I'm taking it upon myself to do it."

Her lips eased back into a smile. Yes, the caretaker was being a bit forward, but she couldn't fault him for speaking out of concern for Ethan. And it was so very obvious that that was his motive.

Besides, Bob's observation that having a woman in his life was good for Ethan only solidified in her mind the idea that Sona's daddy really did need a soulmate. Abby had thought that from the very beginning. Granted, Ethan hadn't liked the idea much when she'd brought it up, but that didn't make it any less true. He did need a woman in his life.

Abby's mind churned. Maybe...just maybe...she could get up enough nerve to mention the notion to him again before she left his home for good.

"You haven't seemed all that unhappy here, yourself," Bob commented, a rare and wry grin splitting his wrinkled face.

"Oh, you're right there," she quickly assured him.

He seemed to be waiting for her to elaborate, and when she didn't, he said, "So, why do you have to be rushing off? When you and Ethan seem to get along so well together."

His last statement contained more innuendo than Abby was comfortable with. Again she felt embarrassed. She and Ethan had been toying with one another. Playing with the physical attraction they both felt. But it didn't mean anything. It couldn't. It was just...fun. A dalliance. That was all. Yet, explaining all that to the caretaker just seemed too personal. Too intimate. However, Abby still felt the man deserved to know the honest-to-goodness bottom line.

She unlatched the gate, stepped out of the stall and then fastened the latch behind her. Then she went to the opening of the stall where Bob was standing. She needed to get closer. To make him understand, once and for all, how things stood.

"I can't stay here," she said, her voice sounding tiny and weak when she'd meant for it to come out strong and firm. She heard something else in her tone, too. Something she couldn't quite identify.

Bob chuckled softly. "You seem so uncertain."

That's what it was! The fact that the caretaker had recognized the doubt in her tone when she herself hadn't, made her face flame.

"Tell me, Abby," he said, "why can't you stay?"

"W-well...I—I," she stammered. She stopped, forced herself to take a deep breath in an effort to gather her wits together. However, actually hearing the question—the same one that had tormented her, the same one that she kept pushing aside—really alarmed her to no end.

Then she blurted, "I have a job. In Slovakia."

Bob waved that notion off with a toss of his large, callused hand. "Jobs are a dime a dozen. You can work anywhere."

The fact that he was able to toss aside her one, good and solid excuse caused her more upset than she was able to bear. That strange, shadowy fear crept up on her and she panicked.

"I—I just can't stay here," she cried. And then she bolted from the barn.

"Well, it's nearly over."

The sound of Ethan's voice nudged Abby from her cozy, sluggish state. She sat in the dark in the screened-in back porch, just listening to the quiet sounds of the night. Sona had been tucked into bed, and Abby had slipped into her satin nightgown and matching robe and had come out here to relax.

She knew she had plenty of problems to work out. The way she'd literally scrambled to dodge the caretaker and his questions in the barn yesterday...along with all the implications associated with that escape

The fact that she needed to tell Ethan about the job she'd procured. And the idea that she really needed to stop this pointless teasing and flirting with him.

But she didn't want to stop! Ethan made her feel so...pretty, so...happy, so...*alive.*

The porch had seemed like the perfect place to retreat with all these troubling thoughts. One thing was certain, since coming to America she'd become a master at evading anxiety and problems.

She sighed at the thought, grinning in the dark.

''What's nearly over?'' she asked, tucking her feet up underneath her to make room on the wicker settee for him.

He sat. ''Our marriage.''

The pleasant haze that had enveloped her until that moment dissolved.

''The annulment papers have arrived?'' She sat up straight, placing her bare feet on the floor.

''Mm-hm,'' he answered, lifting the large manila envelope for her to see. ''All we need to do is read and sign the documents, and then my lawyer will file them. And it's over.''

''Wow.'' Abby didn't know how she should feel. It wasn't like their marriage had ever been *real.* It had all occurred so that he could get Sona out of Kyrcznovia. But still...it was just one more piece of the puzzle that was snapped into place, the others being her job—which was also snapped snugly into place, though Ethan didn't yet know it—and Ethan's and Sona's need of her, which was dwindling with each passing day.

Soon, there would be nothing left to hold her here.

Knowing of no other words to utter, she said, "That sure was fast."

"Damn legal system drags its feet with everything else," he muttered. "But with this it's swift, clean and sweet." He gazed out into the darkness. "Just my luck."

"What do you mean?" The question pitched forth before she even had time to think. "This is what you wanted." She quickly amended, "What *we* wanted."

She saw him smile in the shadows, his teeth flashing in the dark.

"Of course," he assured her.

His grin tipped up farther on one corner, the charm of it making her heart flutter like butterfly wings.

"I was only teasing."

His voice had grown deliciously soft, and Abby felt her blood heat. She should control herself. She had things she needed to discuss with him. The job that would take her away. And now the annulment papers.

She smoothed the tips of her fingers back and forth across the indentation at the base of her throat. "So," she said, the word coming out sandpaper rough, "what do we do now?"

He shrugged. "Nothing. Well, other than signing on the dotted line and mailing in these forms." Another dazzling smile. "Seeing as the annulment is uncontested and there was no sexual contact and no settlement to arrange."

The air went utterly still.

"Kisses don't count."

She tried to chuckle at his teasing remark. He was trying hard to make this easy. Yet she felt as if she'd swallowed a lead weight. Pressing her palm against her stomach, she took another deep breath.

"You okay?" he asked.

"Sure."

After a moment, he stood up. "Let's go into my office and get this over with."

Leaning over his desk, she pressed the black ballpoint pen against the bottom of the official document to keep the shaking in her hand from showing. Her signature was not quite as neat as she would have liked, but it was her full legal name nonetheless.

The pen seemed to fairly fly across the page as Ethan signed the papers that declared their short marriage null and void. As if it never happened.

"Done." He tossed the pen on the desk and straightened his back, sighing deeply.

"So I'm no longer Mrs. Ethan Kimball."

His head cocked a fraction. "Funny, but I never really thought of you like that."

"Why should you?" But even as she grinned and gave a small toss of her shoulder in a show of light disregard, pain knifed straight through her heart, straight through her soul.

"Abigail Ritter," he said cheerfully. "No, no. Not Abigail. Abby. The world's best nanny. *That's* how I'll always think of you."

His words hurt her worse than a knife. They were like jagged claws, ripping and tearing at the most tender and vulnerable part of her.

Why? she wondered. Why was she wounded by what he said? His breezy commentary shouldn't hurt her in the least. She had known all along that the flirtatious game they were playing was just that—a game. She had known he wasn't interested in an on-going relationship. Neither was she. They had participated in the provocative amusement, both knowing that there would come a time when it all would end. That was the very reason she was able to act out this silly game. So why was she experiencing this awful torture hearing him verbalize only what she had already known to be true?

Because you love him.

No! Her silent denial was firm. That couldn't be true. She wouldn't allow it to be true.

Seconds ticked by. Awkwardness swelled and throbbed until she was positive it would burst and cover them both in some kind of harmful, viscous liquid that would surely burn them like acid. She needed to talk about something else, *anything* else, except what their marriage had or hadn't been, or what the annulment meant, or how he'd forever remember her. She simply had to shut out any nuance of an idea that her affections for him were anything more than simple physical attraction—attraction she had been positive she could keep under tight control.

What she was feeling wasn't love. She struggled with the silent protestation, even though no other excuse lent itself as salvation. Loving Ethan just wasn't a possibility. The chaos in her mind swirled and churned as she struggled for something to say.

"I—I wanted to tell you—" She heard the nervous, harried quality in her tone and stopped. After moistening her lips, she tried again. "I wanted to let you know..."

He turned to face her fully, and Abby realized in that instant that there wasn't a more handsome man on the face of the earth. Why, oh, why had fate given him such gorgeous dark eyes?

His gaze was curious, probing as he waited in silence.

"I have a job," she exclaimed. "In Slovakia."

She had meant to ease into the subject. To tell him gently that she would be leaving soon. However, that was impossible now.

A frown etched deep into his forehead, and he was just about to respond when a fitful cry crackled over the baby intercom, alerting them that Sona had awakened.

His tone was soft as he said, "Excuse me a minute." And he slipped from the room.

Abby picked up the documents and straightened them neatly by tapping them on the desktop. Then she slid them back into the large envelope. As the papers disappeared from view, Abby felt overcome with a complete and utter desolation that was enough to make her eyes well with tears.

She would not cry. She would not! She was a grown woman. A mature individual. She had gotten involved in this whole scheme knowing the rules. She couldn't expect them to change now.

"I don't *want* the rules to change," she whispered the assertion. But even as she spoke, she knew what she said was a lie.

Well, she decided, she'd have to continue living the lie. Ethan must never discover how she felt. He didn't think of her in that personal, profound, intimate way. Sure, he had flirted with her. Said sweet things. Teased her. Kissed her. But that had all been in fun. She knew it. And she knew *he* knew it. His lighthearted comments just now were proof of that. "The world's greatest nanny" he'd called her. But it was clear that his affection for her didn't run any deeper than that.

That fact was what she must focus on during her remaining time here. That fact was what would make it possible for her to continue to hide her feelings from Ethan for these few remaining days.

Hearing him sing, softly and lovingly, to his daughter, Abby smiled to herself, despite the dark emotions shadowing over her. Ethan loved Sona dearly. And the little girl had come to love her new daddy, too.

Sona kept saying one word over and over, and that word being relayed through the monitor intercom had Abby going into the kitchen. With her mind terribly preoccupied, she reached into the cabinet and pulled down a child's plastic sipper cup. She then went to the refrigerator for the bottle of apple juice and filled the cup.

Ethan had reached the kitchen with Sona in his arms as Abby was snapping on the lid.

"I'm sorry," Ethan said to Abby. "But I don't know what it is she's asking for. I thought I'd learn a lot of her language. But this is a new one to me."

"Dink," Sona said, looking imploringly at Abby. "Dink."

"Here, honey." Abby offered the toddler the cup of juice she'd prepared. Then she looked at Ethan. "She wants a drink."

Abby gasped, her eyes going wide. She'd fixed the juice without consciously realizing what she'd heard over the intercom.

"She wants a *drink*," Abby said.

Still, Ethan didn't seem to understand the relevance.

"In *English*." Abby was excited now. "She said it in English. She just dropped off the *R*. Most children do at first. The sound of *R* is hard to master."

In an instant, Ethan was as ecstatic about the event as she.

"My little girl's learning English!"

Sona giggled, her tired expression brightening. Abby decided the child probably didn't understand why her daddy was so happy, but she seemed only too pleased to join in on the excitement.

"This calls for a celebration," Ethan said.

Abby went straight to the cabinet. "We need a toast. Apple juice all around?"

He laughed. "Apple juice would taste as good to me as champagne right now."

Glasses were filled and clinked together as Ethan called out, "To Sona!"

"To Sona!" Abby parroted before taking a sip of cool juice. "You know, she'll be picking up words right and left, now. There will be no stopping her."

Ethan turned adoring eyes on his little girl. "This is so great, sweetheart. Soon daddy will be able to understand everything you say. And you'll understand me, too." His gaze glittered as he turned his attention to Abby and asked, "Isn't this great?"

She nodded, but in her heart she realized, in that one dreadful moment, that the final piece of this complicated puzzle—her last remaining reason for staying here with Ethan and Sona—had just snapped into place.

They didn't need her any longer.

Abby sat in one corner of the screened-in porch, oblivious to the chirping of the crickets, the high-pitched croaking of the tree frogs.

She hadn't been exaggerating when she'd told Ethan that Sona would be unstoppable now. The child would learn English in no time at all. Children had a capacity to learn that was staggering. They were like dry sponges, sopping up, sucking in—almost to the point of inhaling—any information with which they were presented. Little Sona would be no different.

Within weeks, Abby knew Ethan's little girl would be spouting off nouns and verbs, and quickly learning to put together simple sentences. From there, communication between child and father would be unlimited.

Abby also knew, beyond a shadow of a doubt, that when she left here, Ethan and Sona would be just fine. However, she had to wonder about herself. Just how long would it take her to excavate this very special man, and his precious daughter, from her heart?

Movement at the French doors had her lifting her gaze. Ethan stood, his hands planted on the door frame. The light behind him cast his face in darkness but emphasized his broad shoulders, his long, lean body. Abby marveled at how the mere sight of him set her pulse to racing.

"Well," he said, "after three stories and a diaper change, she's finally settling in."

Abby could only smile, hoping her desolation and sadness didn't show. The feelings were silly, anyway. But snuffing them out was impossible. The fact that he got Sona settled and into bed all by himself was just more evidence that his need of her was fast dwindling, and that only made her misery worse.

"I think we need to talk," he said.

She nodded, knowing that even though the porch was dark, the light cast from the doorway illuminated her face enough so he could see her silent response. She simply didn't trust her voice enough yet to actually speak to him.

He came toward her, but stopped before he got too close. She was relieved when he didn't reach to snap on the overhead light. This discussion was better held in the shadows. Ethan folded his arms tightly across the broad expanse of his chest, leaning his shoulder against one of the exposed, glossy-finished wall studs.

"How long have you known about the job?"

She felt the urge to retreat. But that would do no good. They had to have this conversation sometime. Now was as good a time as any.

"Not long," she said. "Only a couple of days."

His silence seemed to relay his disapproval.

"You knew I'd been inquiring." She moistened her suddenly dry lips. "That was the plan from the very beginning."

"I know."

There was defensiveness in his tone, and the last thing Abby wanted was to argue with him. In fact, she was in no shape to spar. She was already too close to tears as it was. If his anger flared, or she became too distressed, she just might reveal more of her feelings than she should.

"I just wondered why you didn't tell me right away."

Because I didn't want to spoil all the fun we were having. Because I liked the way you flirted with me. The way you looked at me. The way you kissed me.

She couldn't tell him those things. So she said nothing.

He turned his head, focusing his gaze somewhere out in the darkness of the backyard, and silence settled in for what threatened to be a long siege.

Minutes ticked by, and Abby's agony only swelled and bulged, growing ever more uncomfortable. Their time together would soon be over. She had to deal with that. Get used to the idea. And move on.

So she'd made the mistake of falling in love with Ethan. She'd get over it.

But even though she'd someday get over these intimate feelings for him, she would never stop caring about him. And even though he'd told her before that he was not interested in having a woman in his life, she still felt that would be the best thing for him.

She thought about Sona's visit to the pediatrician and how upset Ethan had been. Once she left, he would have no one to lean on. He'd been terribly angry the last time she'd spoken her mind about his finding a wife. However, once she left she wouldn't have another opportunity to tell him he needed to open his heart to love.

Deciding then and there to chance stirring his ire, she wondered how best to go about bestowing what she knew would be unwanted advice.

"Ethan," she said, and then she waited until he looked her way. "You know I'll be leaving soon."

He only had to turn his head a fraction of an inch to look at her. His broad chest rose and fell as he breathed.

"B-but," she continued, "I have something I'd like to say. Once I go away, I won't ever get a chance to tell you how I feel."

She'd piqued his interest, she could tell. His shoulders relaxed slightly and his head cocked a fraction as he locked his attention on her.

"Since coming here—" her mouth seemed to go dry, but she pushed forward "—I feel that we've...become friends."

Tension knotted his jaw muscle.

"I can't help but tell you again that...you need someone."

"Abby—"

But she refused to let up. "Wait," she told him. "Please let me finish. I care about you. I care about Sona. I know I've made the arguments before, but I'll be worried about the two of you when I leave here. I just want you to tell me that you'll at least think about dating. That you'll at least try to imagine yourself with a woman who can...help you. Who can be a mommy to Sona."

She didn't want her thoughts to go into too much detail about what this other woman might do with Ethan. What ecstasy this other woman might find in his arms. Simply knowing the man she loved wasn't alone would be enough. It would have to be.

"Promise me that, once I'm gone," she tried again, "you'll find yourself a wife."

He sighed. His arms falling to his sides as he came toward her.

"Oh, Abby." He sat down next to her. "It makes me so happy to know that you care. About me. About Sona."

She didn't know what to say. She'd steeled herself for his anger. This calm emphatic response wasn't what she'd expected, so she hadn't a clue what to say.

"You're right," he said. "We *have* become friends. And I know I owe you so very much. I want you to understand. I want you to let me explain—" he hesitated long enough to take her hand in his "—why I can never make that promise to you."

Chapter Ten

"She was so young."

His voice flowed over Abby like heated velvet, caressing and whisper soft, but there was a tension in his words that put her on edge...a disconcerting combination.

"Only nineteen." A taut sigh issued from between his lips. "I loved her." He quickly stressed, "I *did*."

He gazed over her shoulder into the night as he spoke, and Abby couldn't help but wonder if he'd emphasized the point for her sake—or his own.

He shook his head, his tone growing faint as he added, "But we were just too young to get married."

Abby sat, silent and pensive. His relationship with this young woman must have been serious if thoughts of marriage were linked to the memory.

"She'd graduated high school the year before," he continued. "She had a full-time job. She was ready to start the next phase of her life, which was—

in her mind—marriage, children, a home…a happily-ever-after surrounded by a white picket fence.''

There was agitation in his movements as he absently rubbed his fingers back and forth across his jaw. ''Me? I was just entering my third year of college. Barely twenty. Nowhere near making that kind of commitment or taking on the responsibilities of a wife and family. I had too many ambitions where my education was concerned.

''She spoke of our wedding often,'' he said. ''I tried to be patient. Tried to explain my goals in a way that wouldn't hurt her feelings. But she just didn't seem to understand.''

Abby felt his deep, intense gaze on her face, but she doubted that he even saw her. He was in another place. Another time.

''Maybe she understood,'' he whispered, ''but she was intent on achieving her own goals.'' He exhaled forcefully. ''I don't know.''

He leaned away from her, resting his elbows on his knees. His neck muscles relaxed slightly so that his head was rounded downward. He stared at his clasped hands, or the floor, Abby couldn't tell which since his position now hid his face from her view. He heaved a deep sigh. A sigh that told her something was coming. Something big. Something bad. And whatever it was, Ethan dreaded the telling, that was clearly evident. Abby's breath caught and held as she waited for him to share what must surely be an awful memory.

''She came to my room one day,'' he said, his voice grating with suppressed emotion. ''She pushed me about setting a date. Again. I kept telling her that the time wasn't right. I didn't want to hurt her. I never meant to hurt her. But she pushed and pushed. And then she blurted out that she wanted to get married right then. Right at the start of my junior year. I told her I felt it was a ridiculous idea. That we had to wait. She acted like she didn't even hear. She'd work, she said. While I went to school. Our lives would be perfect, she said.''

His inhalation was ragged. "I flipped out. I was so frustrated. Didn't she understand what I was trying to do? I asked her. I was working toward a *degree*. Didn't that *mean* anything to her? I said so many things, I don't even remember all of them now. But what I do remember was turning her down. Unequivocally. I told her I wasn't getting married—to her or anyone else—for a very long time. *Not for years.*''

He rubbed his hands over his face. "She called me names. Ranted and raved. Then she ran out, sobbing so loud that people had begun to poke their heads out of their doors to see what all the commotion was about.''

Ethan went utterly still, and Abby had to force herself not to touch him. Not yet. Something in her told her now wasn't the time. He was too wrapped up in events of the past.

"She drove off—'' his voice caught, but he swallowed and then finished ''—and promptly caused a five-car accident on the highway.''

Abby was afraid her horrified gasp would disturb him. However, he was too caught up in his memory to even be aware of her reaction.

"By the time I got to the hospital,'' he said, "it was too late.''

"Oh, Ethan—" This time, the impulse to reach out to him was too great to deny. She slid her hand over his biceps. "She died?"

"No."

The single word seemed to be rent from him, and Abby frowned in confusion. Then what had he meant by...

"But our baby did." His huge sigh was filled with an all-consuming misery. "She miscarried. And I hadn't even known she'd been pregnant."

He seemed to isolate himself, his emotions, from the present. And Abby knew that nothing she could say would comfort him at this moment. She pulled her hand away from his arm, pressing it flat against her chest, against her heart that ached so for him.

"I was so damned selfish," he vented angrily. "I was so wrapped up in what *I* wanted, in what *I* intended to have, that I refused to listen to her. I didn't hear what she was saying—what she was trying to relay—in those pleadings for marriage. She was in trouble. She was pregnant with my child. She was scared. And I turned her down. I turned her away."

The obvious agitation he felt had him raking his fingers through his hair. "My callousness, my domineering nature, my stubbornness...but most of all my self-centeredness caused the death of my own child."

A single, ragged breath tore from his chest, and Abby was certain he was going to break down. But he held firm, releasing the exhalation with teetering restraint.

Abby wanted desperately to hold him, but not

knowing how he'd react, she kept her hands to herself.

"I vowed back then," he continued softly, "that I wouldn't inflict pain on another woman. I wouldn't let anyone fall in love with me. I wouldn't allow anyone to get close enough to get hurt. I'm just not fit to be a partner. That was clear to me then. Just as it's clear to me now."

In that moment, Abby understood. When she'd first met Ethan, she had suspected he didn't want to become involved because he'd been hurt by a woman. But now she knew the truth. Ethan refused to become involved because *he was the one who had done the hurting.*

The idea that he would forgo happiness, that he would deny himself the love and companionship, the sharing and tenderness that a life partner would bring was overwhelmingly heart-wrenching for Abby. Tears welled in her eyes, inflicting pinpricks of pain as emotion filled her heart, her chest, her whole body. She felt for him. Sadness and regret for what he obviously saw as his callous actions toward the young woman, and the unbearable grief he suffered—then and even now—for his beloved child...the child of whom he'd been unaware until it was too late.

Then Abby was struck with a realization. Ethan had made some pretty tough life decisions for himself because he felt guilty about events that had taken place in the past—*events over which he'd had little or no control.*

"Ethan," she said in the stillness.

He didn't respond, didn't move a muscle, and she decided that he was still lost in his horrible memories. The urge to rescue him washed over her, engulfed her like rising, swirling floodwaters, and at that moment, all she wanted to do was help him break free of the past.

Sliding her hand over his shoulder, she gave a gentle tug. "Ethan, look at me."

He turned toward her, and the look on his face nearly ripped her heart in two. His eyes had lost their intensity, even in the dim light of the porch she could see it. He seemed lethargic, as if he'd been running a long, endless race for ages and he was just plain tired.

"You can't blame yourself," she said. "You didn't know she was pregnant. You didn't know about the baby when she drove off."

"I can blame myself," he told her.

There wasn't anger in his tone. Only candid honesty.

"And I do." He paused long enough to swallow. "If I hadn't been so domineering, Christine would have felt comfortable enough to tell me the truth. I rejected her, and she blindly ran away and got involved in an accident that took our baby's life. I'll always feel responsible. Always."

Surprisingly, Abby understood. She smoothed her fingers up his forearm and then back down, trying in vain to give him some small measure of comfort.

"You know," she began, "we're often told to put the past behind us. To learn from our mistakes and try hard not to repeat them. To forget the past and move on. But I believe that life has handed you a situation that can't be forgotten. It can't even be transcended.'' She curled her fingers around his wrist. ''It simply has to be lived with.''

He actually seemed relieved when he realized she wasn't going to try to talk him out of feeling guilty about the events of long ago.

''I also believe,'' she continued, ''that the person you have become is a direct result of what you have experienced in your past. I believe that's true of everyone. You. Me.'' She cocked her head slightly to one side. ''Everyone.''

She softened her tone as she added, ''If you hadn't rejected Christine, if you hadn't turned away from your first opportunity to have a family, then...who knows? You might never have felt the urge to respond to Sona's desperate need for a parent, for a home, when you saw that television program. And I'll tell you something else...you may feel badly about what you see as your self-seeking behavior in the past, but taking that little girl in when she had nothing and nowhere to go is the most unselfish act there is.''

Abby could see from the light sparking in his eyes that she'd made him think. It was a small light—a tiny ray of hope, Abby mused—but it was there nonetheless. For the first time it seemed, he was pondering his situation, his past, from a different angle.

''I'm not about to tell you to forget the past,'' she said. ''But I am going to tell you it's time to forgive. And the person you need to forgive is yourself.''

With each statement she made, his spine became a little straighter. His brow furrowed a little deeper. He was considering all she had to say with intense concentration.

"We can't change the past." She let her hand slide down over his fingers and she gave them a gentle squeeze. "We can only do our best to make a satisfying future for ourselves and the people we love."

Pulling her hand away from him, she slid to the very edge of the seat. She wanted to be as close to him as possible when she expressed her final words.

"I've come to care a great deal about you and Sona," she told him. "You might be angry about what I'm going to say, but what you just told me hasn't changed my mind. I still feel you need a woman in your life."

Before he could respond, she rushed on. "When I think about the scary moments you've had with Sona, like when she tumbled out of her crib...or the worrisome times, like when you took her to the doctor...and even the wonderful moments, like tonight when she spoke her first word of English, it makes me very sad to think that, once I leave here, you won't have anyone with whom you can share those things."

Meaning to emphasize her point, she pressed her cupped palm over his knee and said, "You *need* to find someone to share your life with."

He looked her full in the face, and she steeled herself for his anger.

But it didn't come.

The seconds ticked by seemingly in slow motion. The expression on his face was unreadable. Was that indecision she saw in his dark gaze? Then she watched as his tongue glided out to moisten his lips. His jaw tightened in what looked to be sudden resolve.

Then he blurted out, "I don't want just anyone— *I want you.*"

Why the hell hadn't he held his tongue? Why had he let those words come spewing from his mouth?

Because he'd had no control over them, that's why. In that one moment of weakness, he'd allowed his emotions to reveal themselves. And now he'd frightened Abby away forever.

And frightened was exactly what she'd been when she fled from the porch.

First, she'd looked startled. Then—very quickly— fear had etched into every angle of her beautiful face. Her skin had suddenly stretched taut over her cheekbones. Her eyes had widened with what he could only describe as sheer and utter dread. Even her nostrils had flared with the fear he'd invoked in her. And then she'd bolted.

If he'd only kept his mouth shut, he wouldn't be sitting here. All alone. In the dark.

While explaining the death of his child to Abby, he'd been plagued by emotions so dismal and daunting that he thought he just might fall into the huge bottomless pit of his memory, lost forever in the horror of it all. But Abby had tugged and pulled at him with her soft, comforting words until she'd dragged him free, back into the here and now.

What she'd said had made sense. Some events that happen can't ever be forgotten…he never intended to forget his first child. And some actions and behaviors, no matter how regretful they were, couldn't be risen above, either. As Abby said, these memories simply had to be lived with.

She had been correct, too, he decided, when she'd
proclaimed that people are molded by their past. He
was proud of the fact that Abby thought his adopting
Sona was an unselfish act. He hadn't thought of it in
that manner before. Maybe his past experiences *had*
helped to shape him into a better person.

"The person you have become," her exact words
echoed through his mind, *"is a direct result of what
you have experienced in your past."*

As he worried over his current situation with
Abby, he couldn't help but feel that what she'd said
was an important key to unlocking, not only the mys-
teries of who he was and what he had suffered, but
her own plight as well.

That fear that had overwhelmed her just a moment
ago had him puzzled beyond measure. It disturbed
him, too. No one should have to suffer being so
afraid. But what was it that had her so fearful? he
wondered. What continued to trigger that deeply in-
grained panic in her?

He'd seen it before, he remembered. When he'd
first kissed her in the upstairs hallway all those weeks
ago. He'd kissed her, and she had run from him like
a frightened doe. And the next day she'd threatened
to leave. Only his plea of needing her had changed
her mind about leaving him and Sona there and then.

His thoughts raced. He'd come to the initial conclusion back then that she was afraid of inti-
macy…that her inexperience with men had her feeling skittish. But he'd soon learned that wasn't so.
After the bubble bath incident—Ethan grinned at the
memory, despite the chaos churning in him—they
had begun flirting. It had been fun and frivo-

lous...and Abby had seemed to enjoy herself just as much as he had.

Maybe she'd been able to relax because what had taken place between them *had* been fun and frivolous, with *frivolous* being the operative word. As long as the flirtatiousness remained on the superficial level, she felt safe. Was that it? He frowned. Could it be that, as long as their attraction had been some sort of amusing sport, then she was willing to play?

Their relationship wasn't going anywhere...at least that's what their trivial game had implied. It's what they both had mistakenly thought. What they both had verbalized. Their attraction was external, easily cast aside when it was time for her to leave. That's why she'd felt safe to participate.

But why was she so intent on leaving?

The lure they felt for one another—the powerful electricity—was mutual, anyone could have figured that out. And Abby certainly wasn't a shallow person. She was kind and caring and extremely concerned about those around her. This whole situation seemed like such a contradiction.

Frustration had him grinding his teeth. He felt as if he had lots of bits and scraps of information regarding who Abby was, what she felt and why. But the information just didn't seem to fit into any kind of coherent picture.

A person is molded by the past.

The concept flitted through his mind again. Could this fear Abby felt be provoked by something from her past?

She'd been abandoned by a mother who hadn't wanted her. Passed from foster home to foster home.

She'd gone into teaching because the children needed her. She'd left the United States... Why? Ethan wondered. She'd left the country after she'd graduated from college and she hadn't returned until she'd agreed to help with Sona.

Did all of America represent a place where she wasn't wanted?

Two words seemed to keep popping up again and again: *want* and *need*.

Abby hadn't felt wanted as a child. And every time he'd intimated, through physical acts or words, that he wanted her, she would panic and flee. She taught English to foreign children who needed her. And he talked her into helping him, persuaded her to stay when she'd threatened to leave, time and again, by explaining how much he needed her.

She needed to be needed. But she feared being wanted.

The revelation had him worrying his chin between his index finger and thumb.

Being wanted left her vulnerable to the whims and emotions of others. Left her vulnerable to being hurt. Heaven only knew, she'd experienced enough of that growing up.

He got up, paced to the doorway that led into the house. There he stood, listening to the quiet.

At that moment Ethan felt he understood Abby a little better. The motives that drove her, that made her think the way she did. That made her care so deeply, that made her need to be needed. That made her afraid of the fact that he wanted her.

Now he felt that the task of a lifetime was set before him. And that formidable task would be mak-

ing Abby understand herself, understand the awe-
some fear that plagued her...before she got on a big
airplane and flew out of his life forever.

She was leaving.

With an odd mixture of sadness, regret and a panicked rush, Abby tucked the plain cotton blouse into
her suitcase, closed the lid and snapped shut the
latch. Lifting the duffle bag up off the mattress, she
set it on the floor and then automatically reached to
smooth out the wrinkles in the bedspread.

She had no idea what had happened to her over
the past twenty-four hours. All she knew was that
she had to leave. Immediately.

Last night on the porch after Ethan had told her
he wanted her, Abby had been completely consumed
by a dread so dark and terrible that she felt it was a
monster that threatened to swallowed her whole, a
monster from which there was no escape.

She loved Ethan. She knew that. And hearing him
say that he wanted her *should* have made her delir-
iously happy. But it hadn't.

Instead, she'd suddenly felt like a little girl. A de-
fenseless child sitting in a pitch-black room, fearing
the mean and ugly bogeyman, knowing he was coming for her at any moment.

The feeling had been more than she could handle.
So she had done the only thing she could: she'd run.
She fled to save herself. It had been an instinctive
act. A natural reflex she couldn't have squelched,
even if she'd wanted to.

She'd burrowed under her covers all night, feeling
sure that something awful was going to happen. And

she awoke this morning with the same terrible dread
weighing heavy in her stomach. So she decided she
had to leave. She *had* to go. And her teaching assignment in Slovakia was the perfect escape.

Ethan had accepted the news this morning very
well, considering the way she had left him so
abruptly last night. He hadn't asked any questions,
only told her he would do what he could to get her
a transatlantic flight for tomorrow. She'd successfully
avoided him for the rest of the day. So she had her
meager possessions packed in anticipation of the trip
to the airport in the morning.

She'd miss little Sona. Abby's lips curled at the
corners when she imagined the child's innocent little
face, her blunt-cropped hair that was now shiny from
the healthy diet her new daddy was providing, her
dark eyes that grew so large with curiosity, her quick
smile and bubbly laughter. Sona was a beautiful little
girl, and Abby knew the child would bloom like a
lovely flower under Ethan's loving care.

Ethan…she'd miss him, too. He was a man who—

Ice seemed to freeze in her veins. Apprehension
so awful that she felt she couldn't breathe. Her heart
pounded. Perspiration prickled her brow.

"Stop." She pressed her palm flat against the base
of her throat, inhaling with difficulty, slow and deep,
as she tried to stop the panic that swept through her.

She had to get thoughts of Ethan out of her mind.
Now. She moved toward the door and opened it.

The glow of the moonlight filtering in through the
bathroom window dimly lit the hallway. Abby
stopped outside Sona's door. She heard the toddler
playing inside. She'd spend some time with the child.

Say goodbye. Abby needed something to engage her thoughts, to help her overcome this terrible torment churning in the pit of her belly.

Pushing open the door, Abby had to grin at Sona and Ethan at play on the carpet. The toddler was trying to balance a block on top of her daddy's head. Ethan sat on the floor, patiently holding himself still, and Sona giggled with glee each time the colorful block toppled to the floor.

"Hi," Abby called to them softly.

The little girl said, "Hi," right back with no hesitation, and Abby was once again reminded of the immense learning ability of children.

Ethan swooped Sona onto his lap. "Aren't you just the smartest little girl in the universe?" he asked, then he nibbled his daughter's ear as she bubbled with laughter. Then he looked at Abby. "Come in."

Abby entered, feeling tentative. "I just thought I'd spend a little time with Sona...before I go."

His head bobbed, but he said nothing.

Sona scrambled from her daddy's embrace and toddled over to Abby, taking her hand. Then the little girl led her to where Ethan was sitting and pulled Abby down to sit beside him. Handing Abby a wooden block, Sona made it clear that she wanted Abby to join in the game of balancing a block atop Ethan's head.

Biting her bottom lip, Abby stared at the block, focusing on its glossy sky-blue color. The corner of the wood block bit into Abby's thumb as she bided her time, putting off the inevitable. She'd come in here to be with Sona, but there would be no interacting with the child without associating with Ethan. In the back of her mind, she had to have known that.

Stirring her resolve, she lifted her chin…and collided with the most intense stare she'd ever encountered in her life.

There were messages being relayed in his deep mahogany eyes. Messages she simply wasn't prepared to decipher. Not now. Not when she was already engaged in battling this fearful chaos inside her.

Sona's frustration became apparent.

Letting her gaze slide from his, Abby looked up and focused on placing the block gently on his silky, nut-brown hair.

The toddler clapped and laughed. Abby and Ethan couldn't help but smile at her unfettered glee. It took so little to delight a child. Abby felt a tremendous satisfaction in having a small hand in Sona's secure and happy future.

Movement out of the corner of her eye had Abby starting out of her moment of reverie. Instinctively, she jerked to reach for the block as it fell.

Ethan reacted to the very same reflex.

The block plopped in Abby's palm, Ethan's hand cupping hers.

Their gazes met. And held. Although he didn't move a muscle, Abby felt as though she were being stroked…caressed. Her exhalation was shaky.

Evidently bored with these tedious adults, Sona swiped the block from Abby's hand and toddled toward her toy box.

Slowly, slowly, Abby pulled her hand from where it rested in Ethan's. She averted her eyes to the floor.

He captured her chin between his gentle fingers and applied just enough pressure to have her raise her gaze to his.

"Please, Abby..."

His voice was as soft as the wings of a lazy luna moth.

"Look at me," he pleaded. "Talk to me." His voice swelled with deep emotion as he added, "Trust me."

Fear griped her with icy claws. All the air seemed to rush from her lungs in a loud *whoosh,* but Abby knew the sound, the feeling, were all in her imagination. Still, the fear pumping through her was intimidating and unrelenting.

She had no idea why Ethan triggered this feeling in her, she only knew she felt it. Fully. Completely. In every fiber of her being. It took every nuance of control to remain seated here beside him.

"Abby."

The pleading she heard in his tone only seemed to increase the anxiety churning in her chest.

He was so good, so kind. He'd become her friend over the past few weeks. Why did he provoke this awful feeling in her?

She swallowed, her throat dry, rough, grating as desert sand. "I'm scared."

"I know, honey," he said. "I know you are." His tone died to a mere whisper. "I'd like you to tell me about it."

Again, she experienced that sense of being in a vacuum, of having no air to breathe.

"I—I'm just," she stammered, "scared."

Evidently, he realized she couldn't expound further.

"As long as our relationship remained on a superficial plane," he said, "with that false kind of flirting fun, you were okay. But the moment things turned the least bit serious...the moment we would *connect*, your eyes would fill with sheer terror."

She nodded slowly. "That's true. It's what I'm feeling now."

He empathized with her agony, it showed in his gorgeous dark eyes.

His compassion seemed to bolster her, and she found the strength to fight back the fear. Her tone trembled as she said, "I feel like a tiny child. Waiting. And watching. It's all so...strange. So...infantile. Yet, it's more real than anything I've ever experienced. It's like I know something is surely going to come and...and..." She felt so silly finally admitting, "Get me."

Disgust at her weakness filled her and she looked away.

"Honey—"

The gentleness in that one little word was enough to melt her heart right in her chest.

"—could it be," he continued, "that you're not afraid that something is going to come, but that *someone* isn't going to come?"

She frowned, confused. What could he mean?

"All those years you were in those foster homes," he explained, taking her hand in his, "you waited for someone. Someone to adopt you. Someone to love you. Someone to *want* you."

The panic inside her flared red-hot. Her sight

splintered with sudden tears. She was bombarded by the overwhelming urge to escape him…no, not him…but the memories—*the truth*—he was speaking.

His warm palm and fingers curled protectively around her hand and acted as a lanyard to sanity, to strength. His words stirred her fear, yes, but she desperately wanted to move beyond this dread, escape it, banish it forever. Somehow, she instinctively knew Ethan meant to help her do just that.

"And when they didn't come," he continued, "you shut yourself off. You decided to protect yourself from pain and hurt by refusing to be loved. By refusing to be wanted."

Her frown deepened. Could this terror she'd been experiencing really be traced back to something so simple? she wondered.

He was right about their flirting. She'd found it quite enjoyable. She guessed that was because she had expected the playfulness to be quite forgettable. Oh, but how quickly she'd realized that idea was nothing but dead wrong.

She'd fallen in love with Ethan. Fallen into a deep chasm of emotion from which there was no escape. And that's when the panic and fear in her really rose to such unbearable heights.

"I want you, Abby," he said. "I love you. And even if you run away from me, what I'm feeling for you isn't going to change."

She was amazed that on the outside she seemed so calm, when on the inside she was a mass of chaotic hysteria. *The monster is coming,* a puerile voice in her mind kept chanting. *It's going to get you. Run. Run!*

But the love she felt for Ethan was like a tiny beacon in the ebony blackness of her thoughts. It was almost as if he'd opened that imaginary door that the little girl in her feared, and the black and empty space behind it, the space that so terrified her wasn't empty. Ethan filled that doorway...with his hand outstretched to her.

He squeezed her hand with gentle pressure. "You made me see that I was meant to learn from my past mistakes...not atone for them forever. Before you came into my life, I was half a person. I have a feeling that maybe you've felt the same way." His voice softened as he suggested, "Together, we can be whole."

Oh, Lord, how she wanted to feel complete. She wanted to be loved. To know love. To give love. Oh, how she wanted to be wanted!

The lump in her throat made it nearly impossible to speak, but she was determined to tell him how she felt.

"Ethan—" his name came out sounding as scratchy as steel wool "—I love you."

He tugged her onto his lap and she snuggled her face into the crook of his neck. He smelled good. Like warm citrus. Like security. Like love.

"I love you, too," he whispered against her hair. "More than words can express."

Pushing against his chest, she looked at him, wide-eyed. "But what about the plane ticket for tomorrow?"

His face screwed into a sheepish expression.

"There is no plane ticket for tomorrow." He smoothed his index finger down the length of her jawbone. "I was determined to tell you how I felt. I was determined to make you decide to stay here with me and Sona. So determined...that I tore up the annulment papers."

"You—you destroyed the papers?"

He nodded.

Abby couldn't believe it. She was still Ethan's wife.

I was determined.... His words rang like joyous bells in her head.

He'd been determined to adopt Sona, even to the point of marrying Abby on the spot to make his plans happen. Ethan was a very determined man.

Grinning up at him, she injected as much sultry sexiness into her voice as she could muster as she said, "Determination is one of your greatest assets."

She kissed him, full on the mouth. A kiss that proved beyond a shadow of a doubt how she felt.

"I am determined," he whispered huskily against her lips, "to give you a happily-ever-after. I'm also determined to give you a real wedding. One you'll never forget. You, of all people, sure deserve it."

Knowing Sona played contentedly behind them, Abby relished Ethan's strong arms pulling her tightly against him. They kissed, and Abby knew this was the beginning of a bright future for them all.

Epilogue

"**I**, Ethan, take you, Abigail..."

In total awe, Abby studied the handsome face of the man she loved.

"To be my wedded wife."

The white lace of her gown made her feel like a princess. The love shining in Ethan's eyes made her feel like a queen.

"To have and to hold, from this day forward..."

She thought to look down at little Sona, who she knew stood between the two of them, pretty as a priceless painting in her pink satin dress; however, Abby was mesmerized by the intense darkness of Ethan's eyes. She felt lost in them—no, she felt *found by them!*

Before Abby realized it, she was prompted by the reverend to repeat the wedding vows...words meant to tie her to Ethan for all eternity. Excitement danced in her heart, but she had no problem speaking. Loudly. Clearly.

After they exchanged rings, the minister said, "By the power vested in me by the Commonwealth of Pennsylvania, I now pronounce you man and wife. You may kiss the bride."

The kiss was firm and warm and filled with loving promise.

Bob Davis, Ethan's caretaker, and Bob's wife, Joan, congratulated the newlyweds, having happily and eagerly agreed to stand up for the couple.

Ethan then reached down and picked up Sona. "Hey, there, sweet pea," he said, kissing the child on her silky cheek. The toddler grinned at her new mommy and then hugged her daddy around the neck.

Clasping hands, the little family started down the aisle of the church. Their happily ever after had begun.

* * * * *

*Don't miss out on the next
delightful, delectable Donna Clayton
Silhouette Romance—
HIS WILD YOUNG BRIDE—
on sale April 2000.*

Don't miss Silhouette's newest cross-line promotion,

Four royal sisters find their own Prince Charmings as they embark on separate journeys to find their missing brother, the Crown Prince!

Royally Wed

The search begins in October 1999 and continues through February 2000:

On sale October 1999: **A ROYAL BABY ON THE WAY** by award-winning author **Susan Mallery** (Special Edition)

On sale November 1999: **UNDERCOVER PRINCESS** by bestselling author **Suzanne Brockmann** (Intimate Moments)

On sale December 1999: **THE PRINCESS'S WHITE KNIGHT** by popular author **Carla Cassidy** (Romance)

On sale January 2000: **THE PREGNANT PRINCESS** by rising star **Anne Marie Winston** (Desire)

On sale February 2000: **MAN...MERCENARY...MONARCH** by top-notch talent **Joan Elliott Pickart** (Special Edition)

ROYALLY WED
Only in—
SILHOUETTE BOOKS

Available at your favorite retail outlet.

Silhouette®

Visit us at www.romance.net

SSERW

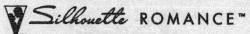

**Start celebrating Silhouette's 20th anniversary
with these 4 special titles by
New York Times bestselling authors**

*Fire and Rain**
by Elizabeth Lowell

King of the Castle
by Heather Graham Pozzessere

*State Secrets**
by Linda Lael Miller

*Paint Me Rainbows**
by Fern Michaels

On sale in December 1999

Plus, a special free book offer inside each title!

Available at your favorite retail outlet
Also available on audio from Brilliance.

Silhouette®
™ *Where love comes alive*™

Visit us at www.romance.net   PSNYT_R